MANIFESTING DESTINY

MANIFESTING DESTINY

Suzanne Purewal

Purewal Publishing, LLC

Noblesville

Published by
Purewal Publishing, LLC
176 W. Logan Street #105
Noblesville, Indiana 46060-1437
www.suzannepurewal.com

This book is a work of fiction. Names, characters, places, and incidents either are products of the author's imagination or are used fictitiously. Any resemblance to actual persons, living or dead, events, or locales is entirely coincidental.

Cover Art and Design by Joseph S. Anderson – TheForgottenArtist.com

Author Photograph by Hether Miles – hethermilesphotography.com

ISBN: 978-0-9829048-8-6 (print version)

ISBN: 978-0-9829048-9-3 (e-book version)

Library of Congress Card Catalog Number: 2017914892

Printed in the United States of America

To My Spiritual Advisors, Tim and Victoria,
For guiding and encouraging me through the tough times

OTHER TITLES BY SUZANNE PUREWAL

Embracing Destiny
Challenging Destiny
From 14 to 41
Mis-Matched to Miss Matched
Finally! An Unexpected Love Story

PROLOGUE

S IX Months Ago – Blissfully unaware of what had transpired back home, in Clear Brook, New York, Sara Taylor embarked on a tropical adventure with a man she barely knew. Phil Potter was intriguing and unlike any man she had ever known. He was an older, muscular man with calloused hands, dirty blond hair, and azure blue eyes.

Sara had run away from her chaotic life in Clear Brook and had driven aimlessly to the Adirondacks. Amidst the mountains and lakes, the brown-haired, blue-eyed beauty planned to do some soul searching for guidance and clarity. However, fate intervened and threw Phil Potter in her path instead. And for some inexplicable reason, Sara felt compelled to accompany him on a trip to Hawaii.

Shortly after Phil's private jet landed in Hawaii, Sara learned of the horrific events that occurred while she was on her self-imposed sabbatical. Her best friends, Laura Delaney-Lombardi and Anna Cristo, had been shot. Anna Cristo did not survive. She was murdered in a drive-by shooting, in broad daylight, on the steps of St. Peter's Catholic Church. Several others were wounded or killed. It was unfathomable.

Sara was devastated and wanted to return home immediately. She chastised herself for running away and taking a trip while everyone else was going through such a horrendous ordeal. She was beside herself in grief.

However, Laura convinced Sara to remain in Hawaii. There was nothing for Sara to do in New York. She had already missed

Anna's funeral. Everyone else was out of the hospital and recovering at home.

Initially, the guilt of not being there and the guilt of surviving weighed heavily upon her. And what was worst of all was the realization that no one needed her to help pick up the pieces. Laura had her husband, John, and a baby on the way. Her former fiancé, Joe Lazaro, was completely absorbed with getting to know his estranged daughter, Flora. And Joe's mother, Rose Lazaro, would keep an eye on them all. Sara felt unneeded and unwanted.

Phil offered to find a grief counselor or support group for Sara. She declined. As a result, Phil became her de facto support system. He knew the job would be difficult, but he was more than willing to tackle it. He loved challenges. And there was something about this woman that drew him to her.

For two weeks, Sara flip-flopped between grief and anger. She struggled to deal with the betrayal and lies of her former fiancé, a cancelled wedding, and the death of one of her closest friends.

At first, Phil's constant positive attitude and suggestions of meditation annoyed her. She sulked and brooded. She walked away from him repeatedly and spent a great deal of time alone on the beach.

Finally, one night he confronted her. "So, how's all that anger and negativity working out for you?"

Sara pushed her hair behind her ears, crossed her arms, and furrowed her brow.

Phil said, "I'm being serious. How long are you going to mope around feeling sorry for yourself? You're not the only one in the world with problems, you know."

She hated to admit that he was right. And she wondered why he put up with her lousy attitude. Sara was disgusted with her immature behavior. But she was stuck and could not get out of this rut by herself.

He continued, "You need to get over yourself, Sara. You've

been in the woe-is-me mode for long enough. It's high time that you get back into the land of the living. What do you have to lose?"

She realized it was time to constructively deal with all of her problems. "Okay."

Forcing her to spell things out, he asked, "Okay, what?"

She admitted, "I'm stuck. I'm tired of being depressed and angry all the time. But I don't know what to do."

Taking her hand in his, he said, "I went through something similar after my wife died of cancer. I can help you. Trust me."

Sara's head and emotions were in turmoil. However, for some reason, she knew she could trust Phil. She acquiesced, "Okay. I'll trust you. Please help me."

His blue eyes sparkled. "Atta girl!"

Phil instructed Sara how to meditate. He was very patient and understanding. He taught her how to work through the sadness, anger, pain, and angst that had welled up. He emphasized the need to live in the moment and not worry about the past or about tomorrow.

Sara struggled. Her life had been extremely structured. She had plans for everything in her life. She had never allowed her mind to rest.

Over time, with Phil as her guide, Sara focused on getting back to basics. He was a good influence on her. She worried less about the things over which she had no control. She began to enjoy herself and her surroundings. Eventually, she appreciated the extraordinary effort Phil was making, all so that she could find herself and make herself whole again.

Phil had purchased a gorgeous, private bungalow on the Big Island of Hawaii. It served as a relaxing retreat, a perfect tropical hideaway. He and Sara walked on their private beach and watched the sun set on the Pacific Ocean nightly.

They took different excursions each day. Some were simple sightseeing jaunts. Other days, they learned about the islands and the culture. Often times, they hiked with no set destination. However, one hike in particular made a profound impact on her.

As they hiked into a lush tropical forest, Phil covered Sara's eyes with his hands.

She stopped walking. "What are you doing?"

He encouraged, "Trust me."

"But ..."

He interrupted, "Have I ever steered you wrong?"

Enjoying how his hands felt on her skin, Sara answered, "No."

Phil instructed, "Take a deep cleansing breath."

She inhaled and exhaled.

"Again."

She complied.

Phil smiled. "Good. Tell me what you hear."

His warm breath on her neck gave her goosebumps. Distracted, she replied, "The wind."

He moved closer to her until his body pressed against Sara's back. He whispered in her ear. "Relax."

Sara's mind was far from relaxed. A million thoughts ran through her head. *He's always telling me to relax. How can I relax with his body pressed against mine? Maybe I should just turn around and attack him. God, I want him so badly. And I want so much more from him. But maybe he doesn't feel the same way. Maybe I've turned him off with all of my whining and moping around. Hell, I wouldn't want to be with me. How can I think he would want to be with me? Ugh. I'm freaking hopeless.*

Sara felt Phil's hands on her shoulders. He was massaging them. His thumbs kneaded her upper back before returning to her shoulders. Then he massaged her neck.

She softly purred, "Mmm ..."

Unaware of her inner turmoil, he gently coaxed, "Aside from the wind, what do you hear?"

She heard her heart beating faster. She wondered if he could feel it. Dreamily, she responded, "Birds."

"Good." Phil urged, "Now, just listen to the rhythm of nature."

Something inside of her woke up. *Listen to the rhythm of nature. Duh!*

At that moment, things began to change and click in her head. She had become so accustomed to her regimented and carefully-planned life, she had all but forgotten the things that used to inspire and motivate her.

Nature inspired her. Hiking and exploring new and exciting places motivated her. And taking a slew of pictures along the way made her happy and content.

I can't believe it! I'm in one of the most beautiful places on earth, and I'm missing it! I'm so wrapped up in my own mixed-up mind, I'm missing out on incredible experiences.

She muttered, "I am *so* stupid."

Phil did not comment as he stepped away from her.

With her eyes still closed, she became quiet and concentrated solely on her surroundings.

Phil positioned himself in front of her and sat on a large boulder. Curious, he studied her.

She thought, *I hear the rustling of the leaves. And there are birds chirping and warbling. There are so many different songs. I wonder. How many bird species are out here? Can different species understand one another? Or does each species have its own language? I need to remember to look that up.*

She felt the strong breeze on her face. It whipped her hair around.

Phil observed her, curious about what she was thinking. He exhaled sharply. *Despite her flaws, mood swings, and imperfections, I've fallen for her. God, help me. Man, oh, man, she's beautiful. She's sexy as hell. And most of the time, she doesn't even realize it. She sure is something.*

Sara turned left. Then she turned to her right. Her eyes were still shut.

Phil was amused by her actions and changing facial expressions. *Underneath that fragile exterior is a powerful, passionate woman. I know it. I can feel it. And I want her in my life. Oh, who am I trying to kid? I need her in my life. And I'm going to do whatever it takes to make sure that happens.*

Sara inhaled the fragrant, tropical air. *When the wind blows from the left, I smell plumeria. If it blows from the right, I smell ... gardenias.*

When she opened her eyes, Phil was sitting patiently, smiling.

She asked, "What?"

Glancing at his watch, he commented, "You've been lost in thought for almost thirty minutes."

Astonished, she replied, "No!"

"Yes."

"It couldn't have been that long."

Standing up, he laughed. "If you say so. Are you done, or do you want to keep going?"

Excited to continue, she answered, "I want to keep going! Something finally clicked."

Joining her on the path, he said, "I'm really glad to hear that."

They resumed walking down the trail.

Phil asked, "You were doing more than listening, weren't you?"

Looking around with fresh eyes, she answered, "Uh huh. Once I closed my eyes, my other senses heightened. Thank you."

"For what?"

Sara replied, "For putting up with my stupid crazy moods and temper tantrums. You must have wanted to kick my ass to the curb a hundred times. I know I would have gotten tired of me a long time ago."

Joking, he responded, "It was more like a thousand times. But who's counting?"

Sara scrunched up her face and stuck out her tongue.

Phil commented, "There's that feisty girl I've come to know and love."

Pretending it bothered her, Sara uttered, "Ugh!"

Phil snickered.

Taking on a more serious tone, Sara said, "Really, Phil, thank you for helping me to find the 'old' me again."

Phil was going to make another joke, but thought better of it. "You're welcome. I'm glad I could help. It was my pleasure."

Sarcastically, she answered, "Yeah, right."

"No, really. And believe it or not, you've helped me too."

Sara looked at him in disbelief.

Not wanting to get into details, Phil said, "Let's get going. We're burning daylight."

As they resumed their hike, Sara felt the bark of the trees. She marveled at the different textures.

With childlike wonder, Sara grasped Phil's hand and guided it on the bark. "This texture is so weird. Have you ever felt anything like it?"

"No. Can't say that I have."

All the while, Phil thought, *The silkiness and softness of your skin is in total contrast to this rough tree bark. I'd rather be running my hands all over your soft and supple body instead.*

As she chattered on, he admired her smile and the excitement in her voice. He loved the way the sunlight peeked through the trees to shine directly on her, like a spotlight. She had star-like qualities, as far as he was concerned.

His mind continued to wander. *She could be the brightest star in the night sky, if she allowed herself to be completely free. And I would follow her light anywhere. She's really something.*

While taking pictures with her cell phone, Sara lamented, "I wish I had my good camera with me."

Without giving it a second thought, he replied, "We'll get you one later tonight."

"Really?"

Phil nodded. "Anything you want."

That evening of her epiphany, before they retired to their respective rooms, they relaxed on a hammock on the lanai. There was a sliver of moon in the starry sky. Phil held her in his arms. They enjoyed the warm, mutual comfort. There was no pressure or expectations.

She gazed into his clear blue eyes. "I had a wonderful day today. I feel like a huge weight was lifted from my shoulders. And you did that for me. I can't thank you enough."

Phil thought, *There are a few ways I can think of for you to thank me.* Instead, he said, "It was all you. I just helped point you in the right direction."

She persisted, "You know you did more than that."

He caressed her cheek. "I just figured out you needed to get back in touch with nature."

"How did you know to do that?"

"Well, for one, you ran away to the mountains to sort things out. You didn't run to another person. You came by yourself to get away from the noise of your old life."

"Huh."

Phil shared, "I did the same thing several years ago. So, that's how I knew. You needed to clear your head."

Sara felt even closer to Phil than she did previously. *He understands me when I don't even understand myself.*

Sara tilted her head up and kissed him.

Phil gladly kissed her back.

Sara's body yielded. She wanted him. Her hands glided over his taut muscular arms.

The softness of Sara's lips drove Phil mad with desire. He wanted nothing more than to make love to this enigmatic woman. However, he swore that he would not escalate their relationship until the time was right.

Sara's hands were on his chest. She fumbled with the top button. Between kisses, she confessed, "I want you."

He pulled back slightly and whispered, "I want you, too. But we're going to wait until we're ready."

Sara knew she was ready. She continued unbuttoning his shirt.

He gently grasped her hands and kissed both palms. "I mean it. I want our first time to be special. I want to make love, not have some frenzied romp on a hammock that could flip over and send us both to the hospital."

She teased, "How about if I like frenzied romps on hammocks?"

Her sexuality tested his resolve, but he remained true to his word. "I will commit it to memory for future reference. Don't you worry your pretty little head about it. Just not for our first time. Okay?"

Sara nodded. *But hearing you say that makes me want you even more.*

He reassured her, "I want it to be a romantic night to remember."

"I'm going to hold you to that."

Phil testified, "I promise. And a Potter always makes good on his promises."

She smiled and snuggled against him. "Good to know."

He kissed her again. *And that will be one promise I will enjoy making good on.*

They sat quietly in each other's arms for a few minutes.

Sara broke the silence. "I think I figured out what I want to do."

He inquired, "Oh, what's that?"

She declared, "I want to take pictures."

"Well, you've got a new camera. So, you're all set."

"Yes, thank you again for buying me a new one." She clarified, "But I mean that's what I want to do with my life. I want to take pictures in National Parks and other parks and sell them. The proceeds will benefit the parks."

"That's a noble cause."

Sara hopped up and grabbed her laptop. Sitting next to him, she opened the laptop. "Now, mind you, most of these were taken with my cell phone camera. So, the images aren't the greatest quality. But I know which places I want to go back to and shoot again."

Phil listened while she went through the photos.

Sara's favorite scenery pictures were taken during her trip to Volcanoes National Park and to Kalapana, just east of the park. She enthused, "Watching molten lava flow from the Kilauea volcano never ceased to amaze me. Even with a crappy camera, the nighttime shots are spectacular, particularly where the lava met the ocean and created new earth."

Phil agreed, "They are impressive."

Diving deeper into creative mode, Sara continued, "So, today, after you got me thinking about nature and getting back to basics, I thought of these pictures of the lava and the ocean. It was that new earth that got my creative juices flowing. New earth, new life, new ventures."

He nodded. "Mmm hmm."

"I've decided it's time for a whole new Sara Taylor!"

Proud of her progress, he said, "Good for you!"

Twisting her body to make eye contact, she said, "When I was younger, my dream job was to work for *National Geographic*."

Surprised, he said, "Interesting. Why didn't you?"

She admitted, "Because I'm afraid of huge bugs."

Phil laughed heartily. "So, you're telling me you didn't pursue your dream job because you were afraid of bugs?"

She defended, "Mostly. Some of the places they would have sent me would have all sorts of scary, freakishly large bugs, and snakes, and God-knows-what."

Shaking his head, he said, "Those scary things still exist. So, do you have a plan for avoiding them now?"

Confidently, she declared, "I plan to avoid them. I just figured that if I worked for *National Geographic*, I would have to accept whatever assignment they gave me. Working for myself, I can pick and choose what I photograph. And I'm choosing not to photograph bugs, or snakes, or put myself in a situation where I'd have to sit in a swamp or some other yucky place where I'd get attacked by them."

Shaking his head again, Phil commented, "That's a plan, but I'm not sure how realistic it is to avoid bugs and other creepy crawly things. But, if photography is what you want to pursue, I'm behind you one hundred percent."

She kissed him. "Thank you!"

Savoring the sweet taste of her lips, he replied, "You're welcome."

Sara resumed, "I was wondering if you can help me set up a foundation, or a charity, or something like that. My profits would go to preserve the parks. I can't remember if I told you or not, but Laura and I always talked about making a difference in the world. But we never figured out how. Now, I've figured it out. I'm so excited! I can't believe it!"

Genuinely pleased with her level of enthusiasm, he replied, "It would be my pleasure to help you establish something for the parks. I'll look into the pros and cons of non-profit versus for-profit."

"Awesome! I can't wait to get started! I'm thinking about selling prints, of course. But I could also do calendars, note cards, and maybe even a coffee table book."

Phil suggested, "Don't forget, you can sell digital images online too. Lots of sites offer the use of their digital images for a fee."

"That's right! How could I forget that? I'm going to add that to my product list."

His smile widened. "There's no need to come up with every product right now. You've got time to figure out what you want to do. But this is a great start. I have a really good feeling about this."

She agreed, "Me too."

Giving her a reassuring squeeze, he replied, "I'm really proud of you. This is going to be awesome."

Not only did Sara feel safe in Phil's arms, she felt strength in his presence. He restored her faith in herself. He encouraged her to be strong, independent, and happy. That was the greatest gift anyone had ever given her.

As weeks became months, the bond between them grew and strengthened. Sara put her complete trust in Phil. Opening up to him became second nature. She bared all of her worries, her hopes, and her dreams to him. He found himself doing the same.

As a result, Sara found herself head-over-heels in love. Phil was everything she wanted in a man and more.

CHAPTER 1

P RESENT Day – Despite living in an island paradise, Sara was restless. She loved the scenery of the islands. However, it was too hot and windy. The ocean was not the same as a lake. She longed for the change of seasons.

Wary, Sara approached Phil. "Can we talk?"

He sat upright. "Uh oh."

She joined him on the couch. "It's not bad."

He raised his right eyebrow into an arch. "Good or bad, let's hear it."

She acknowledged, "I've loved our days here. Hawaii is so beautiful. The black sand beaches are breathtaking. That one red sand beach we stumbled upon was gorgeous. And I've loved the helicopter rides, the culture, exploring the islands, photographing the volcanoes, and everything else."

"I hear a 'but' coming."

She nodded. "I need a change of scenery."

Phil let out a sigh of relief. "Oh, thank God."

Surprised, Sara questioned him, "Thank God?"

Phil replied, "Yeah. I was getting antsy here. Like you said, it's beautiful. But I need cooler weather and the mountains."

Sara laughed. "I was afraid to say something sooner."

Phil leaned over and kissed the top of her head. "Afraid? You know you can tell me anything. I really wished you had brought it up sooner. This is a great place to visit, but I sure don't want to live here permanently. Where do you want to go?"

"Well, John and Laura are renewing their vows. She asked if I could be there. And my parents' house is sold. So, I need to get my stuff out before the new owners take possession of it."

Patting her leg, he said, "I guess it's settled then."

"I don't want to stay in Clear Brook long though. I was hoping I could go with you to the mountains afterward."

A mischievous grin spread across his face.

She continued, "That is, if you're not tired of having me as a roommate." She hesitated, "I mean, we haven't talked about our, um, relationship. You know, like where we go from here. I guess I shouldn't have assumed we would continue living together. I'm just not sure where we stand on that."

He pulled her to him and kissed her longingly. When they separated, he said, "Go start packing."

She sighed happily. His kisses always left her wanting more. "So, you're not tired of me yet?"

Pretending to ponder the question, he replied, "Nope. You're growing on me."

Probing, she asked, "Growing in a good way or like fungus?"

He laughed and kissed her again. "Go pack. And stop over-thinking everything."

Although it was not a clear-cut answer, it was enough to placate her for the time-being. Truth be told, she was glad Phil had insisted on building a strong foundation as friends before escalating to a full-blown romantic relationship.

Phil had seen Sara at her worst—angry, crying, and emotionally pitiful. And he had not run away. He was supportive, nurturing, caring, and loving. Always patient. Never mean or cruel.

Sara considered Phil an intriguing dichotomy—masculine, strong, a man's man, and yet, on the other hand, he was vulnerable and in touch with his feelings.

Above all, it was the calming influence he had on her that she considered remarkable and utterly unprecedented. With him, her heart felt at home.

CHAPTER 2

S ARA stared wistfully out the airplane window. The Hawaiian Islands faded below the clouds. Escaping to Hawaii six months ago with Phil Potter was the most impulsive decision she had ever made. At the time, she considered it to be a much-needed diversion. She had no idea what a profound, life-altering decision it would become for her.

Now, she was headed back home to Clear Brook, New York. There, she hoped to get closure with her past in order to move on successfully. She did not want any unfinished business.

Sara glanced over at Phil. His eyes were closed. He looked peaceful. It still amazed her that he had become the center of her universe in such a short amount of time.

She considered how far she had travelled, literally and figuratively. Her old career trajectory had been uninspired. For too long, she lived her life to please everyone else.

However, with this infusion of positive energy and support, her spirit was renewed. Her creativity returned. She was determined to follow her heart and do what made her happy and fulfilled. And in doing so, she believed she would make a positive difference in the world.

For the first time, she knew this was what she was meant to do. This creative world was where she belonged. And Phil Potter was the man to accompany her on this wonderful journey. Peace filled her body, mind, and soul.

She pulled out her laptop and fired it up. She opened the folder which contained what she called, "People Pictures." Most of her shots did not include people. She preferred working with the pure elements of nature that called to her.

Although, she felt compelled to take pictures of Phil. The majority of the time, he was unaware of her picture-taking. She loved capturing him in candid moments. They brought out the raw masculinity in him as well as his contemplative side.

She felt as if she owed him a debt of gratitude for reminding her how life was more than rigid structure and business meetings. Life was about experiences and using every single one of your senses. Most importantly, together, they were living life to its fullest and sharing an ideal existence. She was still amazed how he was able to instill a calmness in her, while simultaneously inspiring her beyond her wildest dreams.

With these happy thoughts, she closed her eyes and fell asleep.

When Phil awoke from his nap, he stretched and watched Sara sleep. Although she had been an emotional wreck when they met, he knew there was something special about this young woman.

He thought, *I never thought I'd find someone who would touch my heart the way you do. After my wife died, I was convinced I'd never love that way again. But, then you entered my life. And after only six months, I can't imagine my life without you. You've completely bewitched me.*

The slideshow on her laptop was still going. He saw the pictures she had taken of him. He was overwhelmed at the sheer number of them. However, he was more amazed at how easily she was able to capture his essence. *She has a remarkable eye. If her other photos are half this good, there's no telling what she'll be able to achieve.*

He leaned over and kissed her cheek. "Sleep, my beauty. Exciting adventures lie ahead."

She stirred slightly but remained asleep.

He continued to watch the slideshow. It transitioned from pictures of molten lava, to vividly-colored wildflowers, birds in flight, rushing waterfalls, lush foliage, and finally, back around to him. Although there were a few pictures he missed the first time around.

In one of the parks, Sara had handed her camera to a fellow photographer, so he could snap a picture of the two of them together. That photographer shot while Sara and Phil were deciding how to pose for the picture.

There was one picture in particular that leapt from the screen. Phil was brushing Sara's hair away from her face, something he found himself doing more and more often.

The love Sara had for him was clearly evident in the softness in her eyes and the easiness of her smile. She carried that identical expression throughout all of the pictures that followed.

Stumbling across these photos was akin to finding buried treasure. They provided Phil with unexpected insight. He knew how he felt about her. His only concern was that he might just be a warm body that was available to her. He did not want to jump into a sexual relationship with her unless he was convinced their relationship was genuine, not out of convenience. *If I had any doubt of her feelings for me, I don't any longer.*

He smiled as he reclined in his seat, his mind flooded with ideas of how to make their first time together special.

CHAPTER 3

T HREE young Hispanic brothers sat in a bright yellow Dodge Charger SRT. Their eyes were transfixed on a house, four houses down, across the street. It was a two-story, faded yellow and white Victorian-style house.

The driver and oldest brother, Marco Moreno, asked, "So, you guys know what to do, right?"

Nico, the fifteen-year-old, answered, "Yeah."

Their seventeen-year-old brother, Lou, chimed in, "I don't get why you're not going with us. This is your plan."

The twenty-one-year-old justified his decision, "Because we'll end up in jail if we get caught. I've got the right getaway car for the job. This Hellcat V8 has a 6.2L Hemi engine, with 707 horsepower and 650 pound-feet of torque. She's perfect."

Sick of hearing about their brother's brand-new car again, both teenagers rolled their eyes.

Shifting uncomfortably in the seat, Nico argued, "But you still could drive if you come with us."

Checking his rearview mirror, Marco replied, "No. Me staying in the car works best."

Lou mumbled, "For you."

Marco said, "Hey, I'm paying you guys to do this. It's not like you're doing it for free."

Nico responded, "But, Marco, it just seems ..."

Lou completed his sentence. "Wrong."

Infuriated, Marco yelled, "Wrong? Our father is dead! Doesn't that mean anything to you?"

Nico replied, "Of course, it does. But, this just doesn't feel right. There's got to be another way."

Marco said, "There is no other way. Today is our father's birthday. He would have been fifty. Mama had planned a surprise party. Thanks to the cops, she planned a funeral instead. This is the best way to honor his memory. We're going to make him proud."

Nico and Lou traded glances.

Doubting the validity of that statement, Nico said, "I'm not sure this would have made him proud. He was never an eye-for-an-eye type of guy."

Lou nodded in agreement. "He's right. He wasn't."

Marco shouted, "What? Yes, he *was* that type of guy. What do you think he was doing when he was killed? You guys are idiots!"

Solemnly, Lou said, "He was protecting family."

Marco replied, "Exactly! He was paid to protect the family. Just like I'm paying you."

Nico argued, "But he told us all the time that he wanted a different life for us."

Marco said, "Well, this is the life we've got, like it or not. And remember, he always said that family was the most important thing in the world. And our family has been under attack for months. So, we have to get justice for him. Now, get out of this car, and go do what I'm paying you to do!"

Lou and Nico hesitated.

Marco screamed, "Get out! Go!"

The brothers exited the vehicle.

As they walked, Nico commented, "You know he cares more about that car than us."

Lou said, "Yeah. You don't have to tell me that. He's a real ass sometimes."

Kicking a rock, Nico asked, "Are you okay with this?"

Shrugging, Lou replied, "Not really. But he's the head of the family. Mama's even told us that."

Nico corrected, "No, she said that he's the man of the house."

Lou shrugged again. "Same difference."

"Okay. But, for the record, I don't like this."

"But you agreed to do it."

"I need the money to buy a sweet car next year."

"As long as it's not a Charger like Marco's."

Nico laughed. "No. No matter what, I'm not getting one of those."

Lou reached into his back pocket and pulled out two black ski masks. He handed one to Nico. "Here, you're going to need this."

Walking down the sidewalk, Nico said, "Thanks."

A car pulled into the targeted house's driveway.

Lou said, "Act cool. Look down at your phone."

Nico followed Lou's suggestion. "So, now what?"

"I don't know. I guess we wait a few minutes and see what happens."

Nico checked his social media accounts. He scrolled quickly.

Lou's phone pinged. He swiped the screen. The text was from Marco. Lou read the text aloud, "Stop stalling! Go!"

Lou threw up his arms angrily and gestured toward the car that had just pulled up. He muted his phone and shoved it into his back pocket.

Nico remarked, "You know, sometimes, I really hate him."

Resigned to the situation, Lou said, "Me too. Let's walk by the house. Then, we'll double back. I'm hoping we can get a better idea of how many people we're dealing with by looking in the windows. Once we find out how many people are in there, I'll go around back. You can take the front."

Nico replied, "Okay. But I still don't like this."

CHAPTER 4

J OE Lazaro dropped off his daughter, Flora, at his parents' house. His uncle, Mario, was hosting poker night in his basement. So, Joe, his brother, Tony, and their father, Sal, were going to enjoy some male bonding time.

Consequently, Joe's mother, Rose, planned an evening of baking cookies with her granddaughter.

Joe bent over to kiss his mother on the cheek. "Thanks again, Ma, for watching Flora."

She returned the kiss. "It's my pleasure. You boys run along, and have a good time."

In unison, they replied, "We will."

After the men departed, Rose asked Flora, "What type of cookies would you like to make?"

The six-year-old ran to the drawer where the aprons were stored. She pulled out one for her grandmother and another for herself. She replied, "Can we make chocolate chip and peanut butter? Those are my favorite."

Accepting the apron handed to her, Rose responded, "Of course."

Flora tied her apron securely around her waist. Speaking rapidly, she asked, "And can we make sugar cookies with M&M's on them too? How about sprinkles? Can we put sprinkles on some? I love sprinkles. But, I love M&M's more than sprinkles."

Smiling, Rose answered, "Is that so?"

"Yes! Oh, there are all the pretty colored sugars too. I almost forgot about those."

Concentrating, Flora used her fingers to prioritize her favorites. "I guess I love chocolate chips, then M&M's, then colored sugar, then sprinkles."

Obtaining measuring cups from the cupboard, Rose said, "I guess you have thought a lot about this."

Kneeling on a kitchen chair, Flora responded, "Not really. I just figured it out right now."

Locating the cookie sheets, Rose asked, "But what happened to the peanut butter?"

Flora picked up the jar of peanut butter, examined it thoroughly, and furrowed her brow. "I don't know. What happened to it?"

Laughing out loud, Rose clarified, "I meant what are you putting on the peanut butter cookies?"

Putting the jar down, Flora replied, "Oh, just the fork marks."

Rose nodded. "Well, young lady, that's quite a list of cookies. We better get started."

Within minutes, the kitchen table and counters were covered with ingredients and cookie sheets.

The chocolate chip cookies went into the oven first. The smell of warm cookies filled the kitchen.

Flora sang a nonsensical song while she struggled to mix the sugar cookie dough. Rose worked on the peanut butter dough.

Exasperated, Flora put her hands on her hips. "I think I need to join a gym, Grandma."

"Oh really? Why do you think that?"

Pushing her curly black hair back from her face, she said, "Making cookies is really hard work. I need to build up my muscles."

Suppressing a laugh, Rose said, "Honey, I think you can hold off on the gym for now. Why don't I finish mixing? You can roll the dough into balls and put them on the cookie sheets."

Relieved, Flora agreed, "Okay, it's a deal!"

Rose mixed the dough as Flora placed dough balls on the

baking sheets. Flora repositioned several, making sure they were properly spaced. Rose smiled as she observed her granddaughter.

After a few minutes, the oven timer beeped.

Clapping, Flora celebrated, "Yay! The first batch of cookies is ready!"

As Rose removed the trays from the oven, she heard the floor squeak in the dining room. She thought, *Floorboards do not squeak on their own.*

Not wanting to alarm Flora, Rose placed one hot tray on the stove. Before she could put the other hot tray down and whisk Flora to safety, Rose's peripheral vision caught movement. Her fear was confirmed—they had uninvited company.

As a masked man rushed at Rose, she whipped around and clobbered the intruder with the hot baking sheet. Chocolate chip cookies flew everywhere.

Flora shrieked and ran behind the kitchen table.

Nico Moreno yelled at Rose, "Ow! You burned me!"

She hit him again. The tray buckled when it connected with Nico's head. He stumbled backward.

Flora watched, wide-eyed. "Get him, Grandma! Hit him again!"

Rose tossed the bent tray aside and grabbed the next closest thing—her rolling pin.

When he saw the raised rolling pin, he froze.

However, five-foot, two-inch Rose Lazaro was not one to hesitate. She brought her weapon down, full force. He spun to his right. The rolling pin connected with his left shoulder.

Nico swore, "Jesus Christ! Stop!"

Infuriated, she chided, "Don't you dare use the Lord's name in vain in my house!"

He attempted to retreat. Afraid to turn his back to her, he shuffled sideways.

Rose was having none of that. She charged, and again, hit his left shoulder. But this time, she heard a crack.

Nico yelped in pain as his left arm went limp. With wild eyes trained on Rose, he reached into his right front pocket.

Out of the corner of her eye, Rose saw movement by the back door.

Flora saw the shadow at the door too. Pointing, she warned, "Grandma! Grandma! There's somebody outside!"

Knowing she couldn't battle two men, Rose made a calculated move. Before the man could pull out what she assumed was a gun from his pocket, she raised the rolling pin one more time and threw it at her assailant.

He failed to duck, and it hit him squarely in the head. Nico crashed to the floor with a loud thud.

Rose pulled her cell phone out of her apron pocket and tossed it toward Flora. It landed on the kitchen table. Flora stretched to reach it.

Rose ordered, "Flora, run upstairs, and call 9-1-1!"

Flora protested, "I'm a big girl. I can help."

"Not this time, Flora." She ordered, "Go upstairs!"

As stubborn as her grandmother, Flora stood her ground while she dialed.

Outside, Lou Moreno jiggled the door knob. That refocused Rose's attention. She nudged the unconscious man with her foot and retrieved her rolling pin. She was battle-ready again.

Rose heard Flora talking to the dispatcher. She positioned herself to the left of the door and waited.

As Rose steeled herself for what would happen next, Flora zipped across the kitchen with a bottle of vegetable oil. Before Rose could ask what Flora was doing, the child poured the contents of the bottle on the floor in front of the door.

Flora exuded confidence as she ran back to the safety of the table.

Rose could tell Flora was proud of herself. Surprised, Rose exclaimed, "Smart thinking! That should slow him down. Where did you learn that?"

"I saw it in a movie."

In a flash, Lou kicked in the door.

Rose noted that this intruder was slightly shorter than his accomplice.

Lou spied his younger brother sprawled on the floor.

Rose stood solidly before him smacking the palm of her hand with the rolling pin. "Want to try your luck? Your buddy here didn't fare too well."

Determined not to be bested by a senior citizen, Lou entered the kitchen. Unaware of the oil, he slipped and fell.

Rose stepped back as he struggled in the oil. She did not want to slip and fall and end up fighting him on the floor. She worried he might be able to wrestle the rolling pin from her.

Thinking quickly, Flora pressed the speaker button on the phone and placed it on the table. Then she grabbed the open bag of flour off the table and tossed it, open end facing the intruder.

The bag exploded as it hit Lou's body. A cloud of flour filled the air. He choked as he inhaled some of the flour.

Rose complimented Flora, "Good girl! You got him good with that flour!"

With the enthusiasm that only a child could muster, Flora threw dough balls at him. She missed her target initially, but after a few misplaced throws, her aim improved. She hit Lou repeatedly until she ran out of ammunition. Then, she threw handfuls of M&M's at him as he tried to roll out of the pool of oil.

Lou exclaimed, "Shit! Fuck! What's wrong with you people?"

Rose reprimanded him, "What's wrong with *us*? You break into *my* house, and you have the nerve to ask what's wrong with *us*? You lousy, good-for-nothing petty thug! You're getting what you deserve. You're lucky I don't have my gun on me, or hellfire would be licking your feet already."

Attempting to dodge the flying candy, he swore, "Fuck! Stop!"

Kicking his rear end, Rose exclaimed, "For the love of God and all that is holy! Didn't your mother teach you not to swear in front of children?"

Flora pelted the man with more candy while Rose kicked him again.

Holding up his arm as a shield, he demanded, "Stop it! Stop! Shit! Stop already!"

Flora ignored him and continued until the bowl was empty. She scanned the table for additional things to throw.

Rose read her granddaughter's mind. "Flora, that's enough. I'll take it from here."

Flora nodded and resumed her position behind the kitchen table.

Although the oil, flour, dough balls, and M&M's were creating a messy paste, Lou managed to get on his hands and knees. His backside faced Rose.

As Flora updated the dispatcher, Rose located her cast iron skillet. She felt this would work better than the rolling pin. She wound up and hit the intruder hard enough that he slid forward. His head hit the wall.

Lou was dazed, but not knocked out. He threw his hands up to protect his head.

Undeterred, Rose wailed on his back.

With great effort, Lou managed to crawl out the door. Outside, Lou stood and stumbled. Once he gained traction, he ran.

Holding on to the door frame, Rose gingerly navigated the mess on the floor and exited the house.

As Rose chased him around to the front yard, she hollered, "I'm warning you! Don't you ever come back here! If you do, I swear to God, I will send you straight to Hell!"

He yelled back, "You're bat-shit crazy!"

Closing the gap between them, she shouted, "You think I'm crazy? I'll show you crazy!"

Lou jumped into the getaway car. "We gotta go!"

Hysterical over the mess Lou just made on his seat and floorboard, Marco flipped out. "What the fuck happened to you? What is this stuff all over you? You've ruined the interior of my car!"

Pounding on the dashboard, Lou replied, "I was attacked by Better Crocker and fucking Strawberry Shortcake! What does it matter? Go! She's coming!"

Looking past Lou, Marco asked, "Where's Nico?"

Watching Rose get closer, Lou yelled, "Unconscious! We have to leave him. Go!"

Rose heaved the cast iron skillet. It broke the back window before it fell to the ground. She heard the intruder scream, "Floor it! I'm telling you, she's insane!"

The vehicle's tires squealed as the driver hit the gas.

Rose could not make out the license plate number. However, there was no way she could miss the bright yellow paint job. She also saw the word, "Dodge," on the back. Disappointed, Rose retrieved her cookware and headed back toward the kitchen door.

Flora stood on the edge of the mess, holding the rolling pin against her chest.

Reentering the house, Rose asked, "Are you okay, Flora?"

Lowering the rolling pin, Flora replied, "Yes, Grandma. I'm okay. We sure showed them who was boss, didn't we?"

Rose deposited the skillet on the counter. "Yes, we did. You're not hurt, are you?"

In her bravest voice, Flora answered, "No. I already told you that I'm okay."

Hugging her granddaughter, Rose proclaimed, "That was some good teamwork. Messy, but good."

Flora replied, "Sorry about the mess, Grandma."

Standing guard over the unconscious man, Rose responded, "No need to apologize. That mess probably saved us from getting hurt."

Oblivious to the real danger, Flora whined, "The worst part is that now we're out of M&M's! We can't make M&M cookies."

Chuckling, Rose replied, "Don't worry, honey. I'm going to buy you all the M&M's you want."

"Promise?"

"Promise."

Rose removed the unconscious man's mask. She asked Flora, "He didn't give you any trouble while I was outside, did he?"

"Nope. He didn't move at all."

The young man's face seemed familiar. He was just a boy. Rose could not put a name with the face. She racked her brain as she attempted to place him, to no avail. She turned toward Flora. "So, what do you think we should do with him?"

With her little hands on her hips, she declared, "When he wakes up, we should make him clean up this mess."

Rose laughed. "There is no doubt about it. You are my granddaughter."

CHAPTER 5

SARA still had mixed feelings about returning home to Clear Brook. She had not seen her friends in months. Many things changed over that time. She was not the same Sara Taylor that everyone knew. However, to properly move on, she had to deal with the ghosts of her past.

She was more confident and self-assured. She was hopeful for the future, despite not knowing exactly what it would bring. However, with Phil by her side, she was ready to conquer the world.

She realized that her on-again, off-again relationship with Joe Lazaro primarily revolved around sexual chemistry. That chemistry produced a powerful drug-like stupor that led to an emotional addiction. Now, she understood that their relationship lacked the depth of a true partnership on all levels.

Phil Potter satisfied her in ways she had not known were possible outside of a physical and sexual relationship. When they discovered they had a similar vision of making a difference in the world, everything began falling into place.

The more brainstorming ideas that Sara and Phil shared, the closer they became. He afforded her the time she needed to find peace within herself, to identify her true calling, and allow her to pursue her dreams. She hoped and prayed that that special bond would transition into a passionate love affair.

After Phil's private jet landed, they caught a ride with a driving service to Sara's parents' house on Springhill Drive. Until recently, the brick ranch was the only house Sara had ever known. Her parents, Nick and Chris, sold it to live like nomads. So, Sara had to pick up her belongings and vacate the house before the new owners took possession of the house in two weeks.

Phil escorted Sara to the front door. She unlocked the door, and they entered the foyer.

The house was eerily quiet. All of the furniture and pictures had been removed. Without them, the house looked unfamiliar. All that remained were neat stacks of boxes. Her name was inked on each box in black magic marker.

Phil said, "Home sweet home."

Sara disagreed, "Except, it's not. Not really."

He understood. "The empty house is throwing you off, isn't it?"

Feeling lost, she walked toward the kitchen. "Yeah. It's just weird. I've never seen it empty before."

Concerned, he asked, "Are you okay?"

She turned and looked into his eyes. "I will be."

Phil hugged her. "Yes, honey, you will be. I promise."

When their embrace ended, she noticed a small box resting on the kitchen counter. There was a note taped to the box.

Phil inquired, "What's that?"

Picking it up, she recognized the handwriting as Laura's. "It says, 'Anna would have wanted you to have this.'"

Sara opened the box. "It was the butterfly necklace I gave Anna for her twenty-first birthday." Sara clutched the necklace and cried.

Phil held and comforted her as he gently wiped away her tears. He realized this visit would be difficult for her. And he was determined to do everything in his power to ease her sorrow.

CHAPTER 6

OFFICER Vinnie Varone, Rose's nephew, arrived within six minutes of Flora's emergency call. The six-foot, three-inch tall officer had quite the commanding presence. His well-sculpted physique perpetually tested the limits of his uniforms. On the way to the scene, he alerted Rose's son, Tony, of the situation. Poker night ended immediately.

Rose paced back and forth while Vinnie secured the scene.

Flora fidgeted on the couch.

The investigators and technicians insisted they stay out of the way, in the family room. Flora craned her neck to watch them gather evidence and process the scene.

Tony, Joe, and Sal burst into the house just as the ambulance pulled out of the driveway with the unconscious intruder.

Frantic, Sal shouted, "Rose! Flora!"

Rose answered, "We're in the family room. We're fine, Sal."

Excited, Flora replied, "Hi, Grandpa! You should have seen Grandma! She beat up the bad men really good! We were making cookies, and they broke in. But Grandma hit the bad man with the tray right out of the oven! The cookies flew all over!" She giggled. "She chased him around with a rolling pin and hit him and hit him. Then she threw it at his head. That's when he stopped moving."

The men exchanged glances, then looked at Rose.

Nonchalantly, she shrugged her shoulders and nodded to confirm the story.

Joe rushed to Flora and knelt in front of her. "Are you okay?"

She hugged him. "Yes, Daddy. I'm fine. But I'm not done with my story."

His daughter was a chatterbox. He imagined this was what his mother had been like as a child. He laughed. "Of course, you aren't."

Gesturing with her arms and hands, Flora continued, "Then Grandma and I saw a second bad man at the door. I poured oil all over the floor, so he would fall. And you know what?"

He played along. "What?"

Beaming, she said, "He did!"

Enjoying his daughter's enthusiasm, he asked, "Really?"

"Yes. And when I was talking to the dispatcher lady, I threw flour, and dough balls, and M&M's at him. I was going to throw the sprinkles at him next, but Grandma told me not to. Then, he ran outside, and Grandma chased him away."

Sal hugged his wife, Rose. "Thank God, you're not hurt."

Rose squeezed him back. "I've always told you that I can take care of myself."

Sal replied, "Yes, dear. But I still worry."

Tony asked, "Vinnie, is that what happened?"

Still within earshot of Rose, Vinnie answered, "Yeah. Might have been a robbery attempt. Your mother beat one guy unconscious with a rolling pin. And she beat the other one with a cast iron skillet. The munchkin threw oil, flour, cookie dough, and M&M's at him, like she said. Oh, and your mother also threw her skillet at the getaway car and broke the back window."

Shaking his head, Tony replied, "I don't even know what to say about all of that."

Walking farther away from Rose, Vinnie said, "It *is* funny when you think about it. They were pretty resourceful."

"Nice to know that Ma can take care of herself and Flora."

Vinnie lowered his voice. "And then some. I think she cracked that guy's skull."

"Well, he broke in. So, he got what he deserved."

Vinnie reported, "I got a loaded gun and a high school

identification card off the kid on the floor. His name is Nico Moreno. He's related to Al Fuentes. The kid's father was one of the guys killed when we took down Al and his mother. You remember Al, the guy who caused last year's church massacre?"

Gritting his teeth, Tony responded, "You know I'll never forget that day as long as I live. You don't have to remind me constantly and be such an asshole about it. I'm sorry you lost Anna. She was a nice girl. And I lost Georgie, the only woman I've *ever* loved, that day. We all suffered terribly. Still, you have to keep rubbing salt in the open wound. Don't you think I would have traded places with either of them if I could have? Because I would have. In a heartbeat. I would have done *anything* to save them. And I mean *anything*. So, thanks again for the reminder. You're such a goddamn asshole."

Regretting his tone, Vinnie replied, "I know. You're right. I am. I'm sorry. Sometimes I get carried away. Those shitty anger management classes didn't help at all. Nothing has helped. It's just, well, I miss Anna. I know you miss Georgie. I'm a jerk. I'm sorry. Truce?"

Tony nodded slightly.

After an awkward pause, Vinnie resumed, "Unfortunately, I don't think that ordeal from last year is over. You need to consult with your team. We need them and their resources."

"I've already contacted Sully. He's assembling the team."

"Good. In my opinion, I think you, Uncle Sal, Aunt Rose, Joe, and Flora all need to go into protective custody immediately. It doesn't look like that guy's family is going to stop until their brand of justice has been served."

Holding his head, Tony uttered, "Shit. You know Ma isn't going to go for it."

Vinnie emphasized, "Everyone is in danger, Tony. You gotta do something. And quick."

Rose shouted, "When can I get back into my kitchen? I've got a huge mess to clean up."

Raising his voice, Vinnie replied, "As soon as they finish processing the scene, Aunt Rose."

She yelled back, "What's there to process? They broke in to rob us. They didn't get anything. I made sure of that. You've got one of the delinquents in custody. When he wakes up, force him to give up the other ones. Simple. Case closed."

Vinnie sighed. "If only it was that simple."

Rose shouted at the technicians in the kitchen, "I've got cleaning to do. We've got cookies to bake. Shake a leg! Move it, or lose it!"

CHAPTER 7

MARCO Moreno drove directly to his girlfriend's apartment's ramp garage. He backed the vehicle into a poorly-lit spot, so passersby would not notice the shattered back window.

Lou fretted, "What are we going to do about Nico?"

Marco replied, "Nothing."

"Nothing? How can we do nothing?"

Marco reminded him, "You're the one who left him."

"He was unconscious. I had no choice."

"You had *no* choice? You had a gun. All you had to do was shoot her and the kid. Then, you could have dragged him out. But you didn't. So, this is all *your* fault. Anyway, the cops have him by now. We need to stay away from him."

"How can we just abandon him? He's our brother."

Furious, Marco yelled, "I gave you guys one simple job, and you couldn't do it! And on top of it, you've ruined the interior of my car and the back window is broken! You're fucking idiots!"

"Screw you and your precious car! If we're such idiots, you should have done it yourself, you prick. You didn't tell us she was a psycho bitch. She tried to kill us."

Marco pointed out, "You were supposed to kill *her*. If you had, we wouldn't be having this conversation. No matter what, you need to keep up your end of the deal."

Lou disagreed, "Are you kidding me? You want me to go back? You're nuts. Sorry. No. You just better hope Nico is okay. Otherwise, Mama's gonna kill you."

"Nico's on his own. He got caught. And if he knows what's good for him, he won't nark on us."

Freaking out, Lou asked, "So, you're going to let him take the rap for your plan?"

Without concern, Marco answered, "What did you think was going to happen if you got caught?"

"You're a horrible excuse of a human being. He's our *brother*. He's our blood. He's family. We're supposed to protect family. Or did you forget that, since it's not convenient for you right now?"

Marco exited the car. "So, what do you propose? Are you going to break him out of jail? Because I don't think you're capable of that. There's nothing you can do to help him. If you visit him in the hospital, or in jail, or wherever the fuck he is, just know you'll end up in a jail cell right next to him. I suggest you disappear for a couple weeks."

Struggling with the door handle, Lou managed to open the passenger door. "Disappear for a couple of weeks? I'm in high school. I can't just disappear. Mama would freak out and lose her mind."

Marco shrugged. "Do what you gotta do."

Lou slammed the door shut.

Marco snapped, "And by the way, you're paying to have my car fixed and detailed."

Perplexed, with mouth agape, Lou watched Marco walk away.

Marco entered his girlfriend's apartment. Jenny had given him a key when he moved in with her, one month ago.

The curvy, pink-haired woman, dressed only in a snug T-shirt, appeared in the bedroom doorway. "Welcome home, baby."

Annoyed, he replied, "Hey. It's been a long day. I'm tired. I'm going to bed."

As Jenny approached him, she removed her T-shirt. Her large voluminous breasts bounced with each step.

He complained, "You're playing dirty."

Batting her thick fake eyelashes, she said, "You've never

minded before. If my memory serves me correctly, you like it when I play down and dirty."

Marco licked his lips.

Just to ensure she held his attention, Jenny turned, rolled her hips, and twerked her curvaceous derrière at him.

As upset as Marco was about his car, his plan failing, and Nico getting caught, he could not resist Jenny's generous curves. He dropped his keys and cell phone as his focus turned to Jenny's shapely body.

Within seconds, she literally seduced him out of his pants.

After Marco was satisfied, he checked his phone. There was one missed call and one voice message. He informed Jenny, "I gotta make a call."

"Okay. Don't take too long."

Marco slipped into another room and listened to the voicemail. It was his mother telling him that Nico was in the hospital.

He pressed his mother's number on the screen. The phone rang twice.

His mother answered, "Hello?"

"Hi, Mama. It's me."

Frazzled, Lupita Moreno said, "I'm at the hospital. Your brother, Nico, is unconscious. There are policemen posted outside. I had to argue to get into the room. I can't reach your brother, Lou. He's not answering his phone. No one will tell me what's going on. This is crazy. Where are you?"

"So, Nico's unconscious?"

"Yes, that's what I said. Aren't you listening? I need you to come down here."

"Sorry, Mama, I can't tonight. Maybe tomorrow."

"Tomorrow? Are you kidding? Your brother is lying unconscious in a hospital bed. You need to come *now*. What could possibly be more important than being here for me and your brother?"

Marco lied, "I've got a big presentation for work tomorrow morning. I can't afford to miss it or mess it up."

"Just explain the situation to your boss. I'm sure he'll understand. This is a medical emergency, a family emergency."

"It's cutthroat here, Mama. He won't care. I have to be at work."

Dismayed, Lupita said, "Fine, then. Then come right after. And I mean *immediately* after. And I need you to try to find your brother, Lou."

The lies kept coming. "I think he said he was staying at a friend's house tonight. They had a big test to study for or something."

"Oh. I didn't know he had a test. Anyway, get here as fast as you can tomorrow. And I think I should contact a lawyer for your brother. He's a good boy. I can't believe he got himself involved in something bad. I hope it's not drugs. Thank God, your father isn't alive to see this. He would be furious."

"Gotta go, Mama. See you soon."

Jenny overheard some of the conversation. She knew that Marco was avoiding his mother and lying to her. Still naked, Jenny approached Marco.

Attempting to brush Jenny off, Marco said, "I'm not in the mood to talk right now."

Jenny scoffed. "Who said anything about talking? I'm a girl of action."

Since Marco's father had died, his mood turned dark more often than not. Jenny quickly learned there was only one sure way of improving his mood. She dropped to her knees and worked hard to distract him. Within moments, Marco spread his legs and closed his eyes.

Marco had wanted to stay mad, so he could formulate a new plan. However, the sensations Jenny generated pushed any productive thoughts right out of his scheming mind. And she planned to keep him in this distracted state all night, until he passed out from sheer exhaustion.

CHAPTER 8

PHIL arranged for his brother, Tommy, to help load and transport Sara's things up to his cabin in the Adirondacks. After they finished loading the truck, Tommy departed for the mountains.

Sara's car was in the Adirondacks. She had left it there to be repaired before they flew to Hawaii. So, Phil booked a driver to take them to Mama Lena's for dinner.

Sara had reserved one of the best tables in the restaurant to ensure they had a marvelous view while dining.

After dinner, they held hands as they enjoyed the scenic lakeview drive to their hotel.

Phil commented, "I now understand why that's your favorite restaurant. Everything was out of this world."

"Told you so."

"Yes, you did. Glad I got to experience it."

"Me too."

Switching topics, Phil said, "I have a question for you."

"Okay, shoot."

Curious, he asked, "Are you going to miss your parents' house?"

As their driver navigated the winding road, Sara pondered for a moment. "Obviously, being back here and seeing it brings back tons of memories. I mean, how could it not? I've spent my entire life there. Every birthday, anniversary, almost every significant moment in my life happened in that house. So, will I miss it? Yes. And it will be weird not making any more memories in it. But you've convinced me to look forward, not back. So, being here one last time and moving out should give me the closure I need to move on."

Impressed with her improved outlook, Phil replied, "Good answer."

The bellboy opened the door to their suite.

Phil prevented him from entering and tipped the bellboy well. "I've got it from here."

"Thank you, sir."

Sara entered the enormous suite.

There were bouquets of fresh wildflowers on every surface in the room. The purple, yellow, pink, blue, and white flowers were even woven into the chandelier that hung above the bed. The fragrances of the blossoms were intoxicating. Nature sounds played in the background. Birds chirped and brooks babbled. Phil succeeded in recreating a beautiful field of wildflowers in their room.

Sara was astonished. "Wow!"

Phil asked, "Well, what do you think?"

Overcome, Sara questioned, "You did all of this for me?"

"Yes, I did. Do you like it?"

She hugged and kissed him. "Like it? I love it! It's beautiful!"

Phil cupped her face in his hands as he kissed her slowly, passionately. For a moment, he pulled away and confessed, "I would do anything for you."

Although Sara had heard those words from Phil before, today, they elicited an incredible emotional response. The intensity was unlike anything she had experienced, and it overwhelmed her. She whispered, "I know. And I would do anything for you."

The depth of the love she felt for Phil was unlike any other, despite the fact that they had not consummated their relationship yet. However, she knew that status would be changing shortly.

He swept her up in his arms.

Sara's heart raced, anticipating what would happen next.

Phil laid her upon the bed.

She gazed up at him with eager eyes.

Astounded by his good fortune, he said, "You are the woman of my dreams."

Sara blushed.

Tenderly, they kissed, as their fingers began to explore.

Sara lost herself in the taste of his warm lips and the soulful sensuality in his kisses.

Quietly, he confessed, "I love you."

Thrilled to hear those words for the first time, she repeated them. "I love you, too."

He pushed her long brown hair away from her face. "I want to make love to you, Sara."

Her mind yelled, *Finally! Yes, please! What are you waiting for? Do it already! Take me, now!*

She replied, "You know I want you, too. I've wanted you for weeks."

Kissing her neck, he asked, "Not months?"

Her mind betrayed her as his hand brushed against her breast. "Yes, it's been months."

"That's what I thought."

For a brief instant, she thought, *Oh, no! I didn't shave.*

But that thought disappeared with their next kiss.

There was an undeniable chemistry that had been smoldering between them. Granted, they shared tender kisses and heated moments, but they deprived themselves of the ultimate pleasure that a physical connection would have provided. Now, the chains of restraint were broken. Fantasy was about to become reality.

Straddling her, Phil pulled off his shirt. His blond hair went in all directions.

Admiring his handsome physique, Sara could not resist running her fingers through the light layer of blond hair on his muscular chest.

As soon as she touched Phil's skin, he had to have her. He pinned her arms to the bed and kissed her neck until she squealed in delight. He kissed her supple lips, fighting his primal urges to rip her clothes to shreds to possess what he desired. As his lips traced the delicately exquisite curves of her body, his excitement built.

Phil unbuttoned Sara's blouse and reached underneath her to free her from her bra. He fumbled with the hooks.

She shifted to assist him.

He apologized for his awkwardness in removing her clothes. "Sorry, it's been a long time."

She joked, "Practice makes perfect." Then, she quieted him with a kiss.

He caressed her tender breasts and whispered, "You are absolutely stunning."

Demurely, she replied, "Thank you."

His hands glided lightly over her breasts until her nipples hardened.

Sara shivered. Goosebumps appeared all over her body. She giggled.

Phil loved hearing that giggle. It was definite confirmation that she was reacting positively to his advances. He cupped one of her breasts—for his lips to kiss, his mouth to taste, and his tongue to tantalize. Then, he mirrored his actions with her other breast.

While Phil lovingly suckled Sara's breast, she reached down and unzipped his pants. Deftly, she managed to remove them completely by using her feet to slide them down his legs. He hovered above her briefly before pressing his body against hers.

For the first time, their bare bodies touched, and everything changed.

Sara had literally dreamt of this moment hundreds of times. The hardness she desperately craved more than anything else in the world was pressed against her.

Ensuring there was no miscommunication, Sara spread her legs wider to welcome him. *It's happening. It's really happening. Don't let this be another dream.*

Phil's touch reassured her that this was no dream. She trusted him completely with her body, her mind, and her soul. Making love to such a man would be a surreal experience.

They took their time, appreciating each other's bodies, gentle caress after gentle caress. Playful nibbling here. Loving kisses there. Committing every inch and curve to memory.

Sara wanted him desperately. She longed to feel him pulsate within her.

Phil recognized the hunger in her eyes. He had seen that look in his own eyes in the mirror. It was an agonizing, tormenting hunger that increased day after day.

The time had finally come to satiate that hunger for both of them.

Slowly, deliberately, he entered her.

Sara gasped at the breadth of him. She had experienced men who matched Phil's length, but never had any been coupled with such considerable girth.

Gently, he pushed until she engulfed him entirely.

For the first time, they were physically one, joined completely and unequivocally as one body.

He whispered, "I love you."

Savoring the moment, she said, "I love you, too." She tingled with excitement. Her body quivered.

He lingered to compose himself. She was wrapped around him so tightly, he worried that the moment would end prematurely. Once he regained focus, they fell into a strong, satisfying rhythm.

Due to his size, every thrust connected with her G-spot. His powerful pumping had her moaning within minutes.

"Right there. Mmm ... "

Phil teased her by slowing down.

Sara complained, "Ugh! Please don't stop."

Battling his own urges, he said, "I'm not stopping. I'm just slowing down. I'm loving you, Sara. Relax, and enjoy it. Don't be in such a rush."

Slowing things down at that moment seemed insane. She wanted to give in to her pent-up desires and climax with him. The vivid dreams she had had over the past several weeks of this very moment were on the brink of becoming reality. She longed to give in and experience it for real. She whimpered at this reserved pace.

"Relax." He kissed her lips. "We've waited so long for this moment." He kissed the right side of her neck.

She moaned softly. "Yes."

"Enjoy it." He kissed the left side of her neck.

Her back arched slightly. "Mmm ..."

He whispered, "Get lost in it."

She ran her hands across his upper back and shoulders before continuing up through his hair. Tugging his hair, she moaned, "Oh, yes!"

As he buried himself as deep as he was able, he urged, "Let yourself go, Sara."

Sara was at Phil's mercy. She felt lighter than air and free to give herself completely to him. She was his, and he was hers.

He thoroughly enjoyed the varied expressions on her face.

Sara grabbed his hips and pulled him into her as her back arched. Her moans became increasing louder. "Take me, I'm yours."

Phil's desire would not be denied any longer. He wanted this moment to be perfect. In a low voice, he whispered, "I love you, Sara."

Her walls trembled.

Phil repeated, "I love you."

As she exhaled, she moaned, "I love you!"

He encouraged, "That's it. Make love to me, baby."

Sara groaned and gyrated her hips in reply.

Delighting in her, he repeated, "I love you."

Sara's finger nails dug into his back, as she bucked wildly underneath him. Sweat formed on her hairline and at the back of her neck.

He urged, "Give yourself to me, Sara. Love me."

She moaned loudly as the waves of pleasure washed through her.

He heaved into her again and again as his hormones raged.

Breathlessly, she uttered, "Oh, Phil! Oh, my God! Phil!"

He grunted as his love flowed into her. "I love you, Sara."

The intensity of their union was unparalleled.

Phil had never felt more alive and in love than in that moment. He felt as if the energy of his sixteen-year-old body had returned.

Unable to catch her breath, Sara panted so heavily, she thought she might lose consciousness.

Phil was overcome as well. Never had he experienced anything that powerful. It was exhilarating and thrilling. He muttered, "Wow!"

Sara agreed, "Mmm hmm. It was gloriously intoxicating."

Kissing her lightly on the lips, he said, "Transcendental, even."

Sara saw the love in Phil's eyes. She thought, *No one has ever looked at me this way. I never realized this was even possible.*

Sara whispered, "Wow, Phil."

"Wow, yourself."

"I love you."

Kidding, he replied, "I kinda got that impression."

Ignoring his joke, she gushed, "That was wonderful. *You* were wonderful."

As his hand caressed her cheek, he asked, "So, was it worth the wait?"

Vehemently, she nodded. "Oh, dear God, yes! *Definitely.*"

Not wanting to crush her, he rolled off of her and turned onto his side.

As if drawn by a magnet, her body moved with his. She left no space between them. She needed to feel as much of his body as possible.

Propped up on one elbow, Phil kissed the sweat from her brow as he pushed the hair away from her face. In his eyes, she was by far the most gorgeous, sexy, and vibrant woman he had ever known. He loved her madly. He thought, *I am one lucky man.*

Sara felt lightheaded as she caressed him.

Phil placed his hand at her waist. Sara draped a leg over his hip.

At peace, she confessed, "I want it to always be like this."

He echoed the sentiment. "Me too. This is perfect."

"Mmm hmm ..."

Words failed him. He could not think of stronger or more powerful words to tell her just how much she meant to him. He felt true joyfulness and an all-encompassing love. "You are perfect, Sara. In every way."

She laughed. "I don't know about that."

"I do. You're perfect for me." He held her tightly. Kissing her, Phil said, "I want you to be happy. I want *us* to be happy."

Sara purred, "You make me very, very happy."

He took her hand and placed it on his chest, over his heart. "Do you feel that?"

Sara felt his heart pounding against his chest. "Of course."

"My heart beats only for you."

As corny as it sounded coming out of her mouth, she said, "As does mine, for you."

He nibbled her ear, then whispered, "I want to satisfy your every want and desire. No request will ever be left unfulfilled. Let me love you like you deserve to be loved."

Lustful, erotic thoughts cluttered Sara's mind. Phil certainly had a way of drawing out her innermost thoughts.

As he waited for an answer, he placed steamy kisses along the length of her neck.

Sara's fiery urges reignited. She thirsted for the sensual way he enticed her. Phil's declarations of love were powerful and touched her deeply. Although, she knew that his words referred to more than just sex, she craved their newfound intimacy more than anything.

As if he read her mind, Phil whispered, "I am yours. Give yourself to me, and let me love you."

Yielding to his touch, she countered, "If you promise to give yourself to me, and let me love you."

He agreed, "There's nothing in the world that I want more."

For the rest of the evening, their lovemaking was generous and wholly selfless. Their bodies moved naturally together, exploring and delving into a previously unknown sense of euphoria. Drunk with love and satiated, they feel asleep in each other's arms, basking in the precious gift they shared.

CHAPTER 9

MONTHS earlier, Tony Lazaro's family discovered that he was a member of an elite government task force. The clandestine nature of his work was accidently revealed during an operation that went awry. However, that placed his family in jeopardy. It was then that his family met his fellow team members. Those team members called him, "TJ."

Sully, the team leader, sent out an alert after speaking to Tony about that evening's incident. Shortly thereafter, the team assembled in a nondescript building just outside of Clear Brook. Five men and one woman sat around the long, rectangular table waiting to be briefed.

Three team members were former military. The oldest member, Sully, and Spaulding had served their country as Marines. The only female team member, White, had been a Captain in the Air Force. The remaining members, Lee, Ashby, and Tony "TJ" Lazaro were civilians.

Tony addressed the group, "Sorry we have to meet again under these circumstances."

Sully replied, "TJ, it's the job."

"I just wish it didn't involve my family."

Sully said, "Understood. So, what do we have?"

Tony stated, "Although Al Fuentes and his original crew are dead, someone has taken over the vendetta."

Former hacker and technology whiz, Lee, chimed in, "The guy TJ's mother knocked out is Nico Moreno, a son of one of Al's cousins who was killed when we nabbed Al and Esmeralda Fuentes last year."

White asked, "Does he have a record?"

Lee reported, "No. He's clean. He was away on a camping trip when the original bust went down. Until he wakes up, we're not sure what he knows."

The most physically formidable member of the team, Spaulding, inquired, "How would he know who to go after?"

White answered, "Well, he's a smart kid from a well-connected family. The shootings were sensationalized and splashed all over the news. I'm guessing he did some research. He followed a lead to the Lazaro family and the house."

Tony added, "And with Ma, he got more than he bargained for."

Sully asked, "What else do we know?"

Lee continued, "The DNA gathered from the scene indicates the runner is related to Moreno."

Jack-of-all-trades, Ashby, offered, "It's possible that the sons are avenging their father's death."

White said, "Quite possible."

Crossing his arms, Spaulding said, "Probable for a family of thugs."

Lee replied, "We've got nothing on the getaway driver. Police are checking body shops and glass repair companies for back window replacements on bright yellow Dodges."

Sully commented, "Good."

Lee offered, "There are three Moreno brothers. So, the driver might be brother number three. I'm looking for anything on the brothers."

Ashby said, "Makes sense to keep it in the family."

White asked, "True. But let's not focus solely on them. What about Al's brother, Carlo? Any activity on him? I know he seemed clean when we investigated him earlier. But with several deaths in the family, maybe things changed."

Lee said, "I'll start digging."

Sully announced, "Okay. The rest of you will be on guard duty until we resolve this. And TJ ..."

Tony answered, "Yeah?"

"You don't go anywhere without backup. Understood?"

"Yes, sir."

CHAPTER 10

S ULLY, White, and Spaulding escorted Tony home to break the news to his family.

Giving them the once-over, Rose stated, "No offense, but I had hoped I would never see any of your faces ever again."

Dressed in a black T-shirt, black cargo pants, and black military boots, Spaulding replied, "The same goes for us, ma'am."

Rose gave Spaulding a disparaging look.

He returned her look with a blank expression. Internally, he sighed. From experience, he knew she would give him the most trouble.

Rose asked, "That wasn't a robbery attempt, was it?"

Sully admitted, "No, ma'am."

Hands on her hips, Rose questioned, "Then what was it? And don't you even think of lying or sugar coating it. I want the truth."

Sully cleared his throat.

Rose warned, "Don't make me get my rolling pin and beat it out of you."

Sully suppressed a laugh. He admired Rose's direct approach. "We believe it's part of the ongoing vendetta concerning the Fuentes family. We're not certain if they intended to kidnap you and the child or if it was a murder attempt."

Throwing her hands up in the air, she replied, "Wonderful!"

Sal asked Sully, "So, now what?"

Sully replied, "Now, we need to protect you from the threat."

Rose complained, "When will this nightmare end? I thought that whole thing was over with."

Tony said, "We all did. But apparently, there are still family members avenging the deaths."

Rose pointed out, "You didn't kill that Al Fuentes. His step-daughter did."

Tony explained, "But some other family members were killed during the operation. We think this attack concerns one of the other relatives who died. And the best way to exact revenge is to go after me and my family, like they did before."

Looking toward the heavens, Rose threw up her hands. She exclaimed, "Dear Jesus, Mary, and Joseph! Will we ever be safe? How many family members are involved and want revenge?"

Tony apologized, "We're still trying to figure that out. I'm sorry this is happening. I should have protected all of you better."

Running his hands through his black wavy hair, Joe said, "It's my fault for blowing your cover. That's when everything started going to hell."

Placing a hand on his brother's shoulder, Tony said, "I've told you a thousand times, it wasn't your fault. Just let it drop."

Sully said, "I have a recommendation for all of you until this blows over."

Rose challenged, "Forgive me if I don't have faith in your recommendations. You let us leave protective custody before. You said we were safe then."

Sully explained, "At the time, we believed the threat had been neutralized."

Joe said, "Obviously, you were wrong."

Sully admitted, "Yes, we were."

Sal asked, "What makes you think after you apprehend these other guys that this whole ordeal will be over?"

Rose scoffed. "They can't. Not for sure."

Sully started, "Well, we've come up with a plan."

Annoyed, Rose snapped, "Save your breath."

Joe suggested, "Ma, you should at least hear him out."

With a dismissive wave, she replied, "I already know what he's going to say. He's going to tell us that we have to go back into protective custody and have no contact with anyone." Turning to Sully, she asked, "How'd I do?"

Sully confirmed, "Yes, that's the plan."

With one hand on her hip and the other waving around, Rose argued, "Well, it's a stupid plan. These lousy thugs are not going to force me from my own home. I'm not going anywhere. I'm hosting a party tomorrow. We can't just disappear willy-nilly into the night."

"I strongly suggest postponing the party."

"I'm not postponing anything."

Sully clarified, "You realize that you're not safe here."

Rose replied, "We're not safe anywhere. These people can probably track us wherever we go. So, why should I leave?"

Sully responded, "I had a feeling you'd say that. So, 'Plan B' is that no one goes anywhere alone. That includes the child. Joe, you and your daughter need to move in here. We can keep a better eye on all of you if you're together."

Scratching his head, Joe inquired, "How is Flora supposed to go to school with bodyguards?"

White suggested, "You could homeschool her until this is over."

Joe said, "Homeschool? She's not going to like that at all. She's a social kid."

Rose questioned, "So, we live like prisoners? For how long?"

Sully replied, "For as long as it takes."

Unconvinced, Rose said, "Those sound like weasel words to me. It's a non-answer."

Sully resumed, "We fully intend to neutralize the threat completely. When that happens, we'll disappear, and your lives will go back to normal."

Flatly, Rose said, "The road to Hell is paved with good intentions."

Sully remained silent. This was not an argument he was going to win. Instead, he ordered, "Spaulding, go with Joe while he retrieves some of his and his daughter's belongings. No detours. Come straight back here."

Spaulding confirmed, "Roger that."

Sarcastically, Rose said, "You've thought of everything, haven't you? Except for how to rid us of these terrorists once and for all."

Spaulding muttered, "Lady, we're just trying to do our jobs."

Poking him in the chest, Rose scolded, "Lady? Did you just call me, 'lady?' I'm, 'Mrs. Lazaro,' to you, buster."

Unaccustomed to putting up with that type of treatment without retaliating, through gritted teeth, he said, "Yes, ma'am. My apologies."

Fretting, Joe stated, "This is going to terrify Flora."

Patting his shoulder, White offered, "We'll do what we can to minimize her fear."

Expressively, Rose used her hands as she spoke. "She'll be surrounded by armed men in body armor. Unless you sprinkle pink glitter and pixie dust on yourselves, she'll be aware of the constant threat."

Tony exclaimed, "Ma!"

Walking away, she murmured, "These people are morons."

Tony intercepted her path. "Ma, you need to be nice to these guys. They saved our lives before. They might have to do it again."

Rose shook her head and folded her arms. "Maybe I'll take my chances with my rolling pin and my cast iron skillet."

Sal admonished her, "Rose, these people are risking their lives for us. I know you're upset, but try not to insult them."

Rose announced, "I have a better idea. I'm calling Helen Scotto."

Joe inquired, "Why get her involved? Aren't there enough of us in danger already?"

Rose replied, "Flora's other grandmother can take her to visit family in New York City. Helen told me she was planning to do it soon anyway. No better time than the present. They can leave right after the party."

Sully said, "Assuming Helen isn't on their radar, that's a good idea."

Shaking her head and gesturing, Rose said, "Well, of course it is! Somebody around here needs to have good ideas. It might as well be me!"

CHAPTER 11

MARCO Moreno sat alone in the spare bedroom of his girlfriend's apartment. He had taken it over as his office. A computer monitor glowed in front of him. A cluster of dots floated on a map. Each dot represented the cell phone of a known Lazaro family member.

Spools of different colors of wire rested on the desk. Several unlabeled cardboard boxes were discarded and tossed aside. Empty plastic containers that formerly held nuts, bolts, and screws littered the floor.

Jenny attempted to enter and found the door locked. She knocked. "Marco, let me in."

Focused on connecting wires, he replied, "I'm busy working on something."

Talking through the door, she said, "I can help."

He disagreed, "It's work. You can't help."

Jenny suggested, "I can watch then."

Concentrating on the task at hand, Marco said, "It's classified stuff for work. You can't see what I'm doing."

Trying to entice him, she offered, "Then you can blindfold me."

He contemplated it.

She pleaded, "Come out, and play with me. You can tie me up. And you can spank me."

The image of her wearing nothing except a blindfold excited him. However, being able to tie her up and spank her clinched the deal. "I'll be out in fifteen minutes."

In a sing-songy voice, she said, "Okay. I'll be waiting."

Marco carefully connected the last wires before placing the package in a plain, brown cardboard box. He secured the box with a piece of packing tape. He was pleased and satisfied with his masterpiece.

He cut several feet of wire off one of the spools before he stood, stretched, and unlocked the door.

Jenny waited for him on the couch, wearing nothing except extra-high black stilettos and a blindfold.

He demanded, "Get up!"

Jenny stood.

"Turn around."

She complied.

"On your knees."

Jenny knelt.

He pulled her arms behind her and wrapped her wrists together with the wire. Then, he looped the wire around her neck twice. He tugged on the length of wire that was now strung between her neck and wrists.

She tilted her head back as her airflow was slightly restricted.

With a sinister smile, Marco said, "That will do nicely."

Jenny slowed down her breathing.

Although she could not see him, Marco stripped off his clothes in front of her. He roughly kissed her lips before he retrieved a paddle from the closet. He slapped the paddle against his hand, so she could hear what was in store for her. Fully erect, he approached Jenny. He grabbed her by the hair and yanked her head back. He asked, "You want to be spanked?"

Jenny answered, "Yes."

He implored, "You want me to use the paddle?"

She responded, "Yes."

Marco stroked himself a few times before he raised the paddle and smacked Jenny's ass hard. He admired the red mark that was imprinted on her skin. He traced the outline with his fingers.

She begged, "More."

Marco stroked firmly with his left hand as he held the paddle in his right hand. He hit Jenny again and again.

He paused to admire his handiwork and tugged the wire taut around her neck. He restricted her air intake until she was almost unconscious. Then, he smacked her curvaceous ass so hard, she gulped air.

Within seconds, Jenny pleaded for more.

Hitting her again, Marco commented, "This day is finally looking up."

CHAPTER 12

THE next morning, Sara and Phil got ready for the vow renewal ceremony and party for Laura and John.

Phil wore a dark blue suit and a blue tie with a gold pineapple pattern.

Sara slipped on a floral maxi dress she purchased in Hawaii. She considered plucking some of the wildflowers from their vases and putting them in her hair, but she talked herself out of it. She did not want to upstage Laura in any way.

Kissing the nape of Sara's neck, Phil inquired, "Are you nervous about seeing everyone today?"

Wishing Phil was doing more than kissing her, Sara replied, "Not nervous exactly. It's just weird. For one thing, I'm not staying at home. I'm in a hotel where everything is unfamiliar. I'm not fighting Anna or Laura for the toaster or the last glass of orange juice."

"It's change."

"Yeah. Everything has changed. My friends have changed. My relationships have changed."

"You mean with your ex, Joe."

Spraying hairspray on the top of her head to tame her flyaway strands of hair, she said, "Yeah, but it's more than that. I don't feel the same about everyone or anything here. I don't feel as connected as I used to. It's just weird, like it was a different life or something."

Phil reassured, "You can lean on me if you need to. I'm here for you. There's nothing that they can say or do to change the life you have now. You're finally doing what you want, and it makes you happy. And let's not forget, you've got a great guy—me!"

Sara smirked. "Yes, I do."

He questioned, "Are you afraid they won't like me?"

Curtly, she replied, "Oh, that's a given."

"Huh?"

Applying lip gloss, she said, "I'm kidding. They'll love you. Well, Joe and Rose won't, but everyone else will. Don't worry about it."

"Do you think they'll try to push you and your ex back together? Because that's not going to happen with me around."

Sara hugged and kissed him. "You are the best thing that has ever happened to me. I mean, no one has given me my own field of wildflowers before. And indoors, no less. And no, I don't think they'd try to force me back with Joe. Even if they did, I wouldn't listen. Everything is different now. I'm different now."

He returned her affections. "If you keep kissing me like that, we are going to miss the entire day."

Coyly, she asked, "Is that a promise or a threat?"

He playfully grabbed her rear end. "You know I can't get enough of you. Don't tempt me, or I guarantee you won't leave this room."

"In that case, let's compromise and leave the party early."

He winked at her. "You read my mind. You just say the word."

Looking at the time, she said, "We better get going. Otherwise, we're going to be late."

CHAPTER 13

L AURA and John Lombardi greeted their friends and family in the narthex of St. Peter's Church.

Sara and Phil arrived twenty minutes before the ceremony was scheduled to start. The two women hugged.

A visibly pregnant Laura exclaimed, "It's so wonderful to see you, Sara! It's been so long. I've missed you."

Taken aback by how different Laura appeared, Sara replied, "I've missed you, too."

Laura responded, "You look …"

Sara suggested, "Happy?"

Laura agreed, "Yeah, really happy."

"That's because I am. And this is the wonderful man responsible for my happiness. Laura, John, this is Phil. Phil, this is Laura and John."

Extending her hand, Laura said, "It's a pleasure to finally meet you."

Shaking her hand, Phil replied, "Likewise. I've heard a lot about you."

John and Phil nodded as they shook hands.

Laura said, "We're glad you both could make it."

Sara responded, "I wouldn't have missed it for anything. How are you doing? You look great. And I hate to say it, because it sounds so cliché, but you're glowing."

Laura answered, "That's called sweat. And it's okay, you can say I'm fat."

"You're not fat, silly. You're pregnant."

Doubtful, Laura said, "I'm a sweaty mess who's eating enough food to satisfy an entire football team. But, hey, aside from the swollen ankles, I'm pretty good."

Sara patted Laura's back. "You're just hormonal. You look fantastic."

"Thanks."

The double exterior doors of the church opened. The Lazaro family entered the church together.

Rose fussed with Flora's dress.

Joe, Tony, and Sal tightened and straightened their ties.

Before any of them could say a word, Sara said, "Everyone, this is my boyfriend, Phil Potter."

Rose quickly turned her attention to the new man in Sara's life. She sized him up as a flurry of pleasantries and handshakes were exchanged.

Joe politely shook Phil's hand, but there was sadness in his eyes.

Rose said, "So, Sara, this is the man who has kept you away from home for months on end?"

Sara replied, "It had nothing to do with Phil. I've been busy and haven't had time to come home. He's super-supportive and has helped me see that I don't have to spend my life pleasing other people."

Rose criticized, "Huh! So, you're abandoning all of your loved ones and your responsibilities to please yourself? Interesting. Laura tells me you refused to be the baby's godmother."

On the defensive, Sara explained, "I'm not abandoning anyone. And I didn't refuse. I just told Laura that since I won't be living here anymore, it probably would make more sense to pick someone else. So, she picked her cousin, Mary."

With a disapproving look, Rose replied, "Sara, dear, I'm not buying what you're trying to sell me. I think you didn't want to share godparent duties with my Joey."

Joe attempted to weigh in, "Ma ..."

Dismissively, Rose said, "Be quiet, Joey. I'm handling this."

Calmly, Sara stated, "I'm sorry that you feel that way, Mrs. Lazaro. But I'm happy. I'm doing what I've always wanted to do. I'm concentrating on my photography. I'm going to take pictures in all of the National Parks and sell the photos. The proceeds are going to help preserve the parks. Phil and I are going to start a foundation for that purpose."

Rose inquired, "And what are you going to do when this whole thing doesn't work out like you planned?"

With confidence, Sara said, "I'm going to be positive and not worry about it. Whatever happens, happens."

Crossing her arms, Rose said, "So you think you'll be happy living an artsy Bohemian life, traipsing from park to park, taking pictures? It's ridiculous. I think you need a better plan."

Curtly, Sara answered, "That's your opinion. And you're entitled to it. I'm satisfied with our plan."

Before Rose could comment further, Father Francis joined them. "Everyone, it's time to start. Please take your places."

Sara murmured, "Thank God."

One by one, they turned and walked down the center aisle of the church and took their places in the pews.

Sitting down, Phil said, "You weren't kidding about her. She's brutal."

Sara whispered, "She was just getting warmed up."

"Now I understand why you were running away from these people."

On the other side of the aisle, Joe commented, "Sara sure has changed."

Rose replied, "I'm not sure it's for the better."

Joe commented, "Ma, if she's happy, I'm happy for her."

"No, you're not. Don't lie in church. You'll go to Hell."

Joe thought, *I'm already in Hell, Ma. I've been here for months.*

CHAPTER 14

A FTER a heartfelt renewal of vows, family members and friends migrated to the Lazaros' house for the party. Laura's parents, Tom and Terri Delaney, had intended to rent a venue for the occasion, but Rose would not hear of it. She insisted on hosting.

It was a small gathering, by Lazaro standards. Laura and John had small families. The remaining attendees were firefighters and EMTs who worked with John.

The members of the Lazaro family's protection team were introduced as Sal's relatives who were visiting from California.

Sara thought the visiting relatives looked suspicious. She had spent many years with the Lazaro family. She had never seen nor heard of any California relatives. And she noted none of them appeared Italian. Nevertheless, she did her best to mingle and avoid Rose and Joe.

The men decided to play bocce. Phil was invited to participate, and he agreed.

Laura asked Sara, "Want to go inside for a few minutes to chat?"

Wanting to get away from Rose and Joe, she answered, "Yes."

They walked through the back door and entered the kitchen. After Laura shut the door, she asked, "How are things with you?"

Sara replied, "I've never been better."

Laura commented, "I can see that. You're love-struck. And the way you stood up to Mrs. Lazaro at the church was incredible."

Proudly, Sara declared, "It's the new me!"

Waddling to the refrigerator, Laura said, "I love the new you. Phil seems to have brought out the best in you."

Standing at the window, Sara gazed lovingly in Phil's direction. She gushed, "He has. He's absolutely, positively wonderful!"

Pouring herself a glass of water, Laura stated, "I feel like I should prepare myself for you to break into a song and dance number for a musical or something. I've never seen you this starry-eyed before. It's odd, to tell you the truth."

"I know! It's amazing!"

Laura rolled her eyes.

Playing the part, Sara burst into song, "I feel pretty! Oh, so pretty! I feel pretty and witty and bright! And I pity any girl who isn't me tonight! La la la la la la la la!" She twirled and circled around Laura twice.

Laura closed her eyes. "Me and my big mouth. Of course, you'd go with *West Side Story*. Are you trying to make a pregnant woman dizzy? Stop!"

Sara giggled. "Sorry." More quietly, she continued, "La la la la la la la la!"

Tilting her head, Laura pretended to examine Sara. "Are you on drugs or something?"

Sara laughed so hard, she snorted. "No!"

Laura teased, "You're not smoking anything or taking that medical marijuana?"

"Oh, my God! No! I'm fine."

Laura joked, "Maybe he's slipping something to you that you don't know about."

Sara defended, "No. He's a good guy."

Holding her hands up, Laura said, "Okay, I believe you."

"Seriously, Laura. All head-over-heels love aside, he's an honest, trustworthy man who cares about me."

Laura nodded.

Sara continued, "He got me to see that all of the decisions I've made my whole life were based on other people's opinions or to live up to their expectations. I lost myself in the process. I haven't felt this good in my own skin in a long, long time."

Leaning against the counter, Laura said, "I can see that. I'm even catching glimpses of the idealistic twelve-year-old version of you."

"We had lots of dreams back then."

"Yes, we did."

"The sky was the limit."

Stretching her back, Laura said, "I remember. Guess I got off-track too."

Sara said, "I tried to justify it as 'growing up.' But now, I see otherwise. I'm having a ball taking pictures. I really missed it. And Phil and I are going to create a foundation for the National Parks. I love that he shares my dream of making a difference."

Laura said, "I know. I'm so jealous!"

"There's nothing stopping you from doing it with us."

Rubbing her stomach, Laura answered, "You're funny. I've got a baby on the way and a firefighter husband to deal with. Globetrotting isn't exactly in the cards right now."

"You do have a point there."

Fishing, Laura asked, "So, when are you and Phil getting married?"

"Ha. Ha. We're not even engaged. Who knows? Maybe we'll end up eloping on a mountain or on the side of a volcano somewhere."

"If you do, make sure you send me video or at least pictures!"

Sara stated, "I will."

Shaking her head, Laura said, "I just can't believe the change in you."

Sara responded, "It's for the better. The craziness with Joe, and his daughter, and his mother was just eating me up inside. Sort of toxic in a way. Phil helped me realize that."

"Huh."

Sara paused. "You know, it's really weird being here in this house."

Laura sympathized, "I can only imagine. The last time you were here ..."

"Was my disaster of a wedding shower. It seems like so long ago."

Laura agreed, "It's been months."

"But it feels like a lifetime. I've experienced so much since I met Phil. It's unbelievable."

"I'm so happy for you, Sara."

"Thank you. He's so kind and warm and caring. He's perfect."

Laura remarked, "He's perfect? That's so funny."

"Why?"

Rattling off reasons, Laura said, "Physically, he's not your type. He's short, and blond, and definitely looks blue collar. You usually go for the nerdy, white collar guys. He's no pencil-pusher. He's built like a linebacker. And I'm sorry, but I have to say it, he's a lot older than you."

Acknowledging Laura's points, Sara replied, "I know, I know. He's like the opposite of my usual type. But I'm older and more mature now."

Laura teased, "Yeah, you're *so* mature."

Sara stuck out her tongue.

Laura followed suit and stuck out her tongue at Sara. "And, in less than five seconds, you've proven my point!"

Sara reverted back to singing. "La la la la la la la la!"

Both women laughed.

Sara said, "Okay, I'll be serious for a minute. All of those things don't mean anything in the long run. I haven't even noticed the age difference."

Probing, Laura asked, "Are you sure it's not a daddy complex thing?"

Amazed Laura went there, Sara replied, "I'm positive, it's not! He's not a father figure to me. I'll admit that he does provide stability and security. But that's what a life partner does. It's not a weird father thing."

Unconvinced, Laura said, "If you say so."

Sara insisted, "I *do* say so! If anything, I see him more as a stallion."

"Oh, geez! Is that your way of telling me that he's hung like a horse?"

Sara nodded assuredly. "You have no idea. And then, there's his stamina ..."

Laura held up her hands. "Whoa! Way too much information. I don't need to know any more than that."

Both women laughed.

Sara commented, "I miss this."

Laura concurred, "Me too. Just don't make me laugh anymore. I'll have to pee."

"Okay. No more laughing."

"Thanks."

Sara said, "I have to tell you, since I left six months ago, my life has been like a dream. And I never want to wake up from it."

"Hopefully, you won't ever have to. So, I take it from your stallion and stamina comments that things have progressed from the friend zone."

Sara blushed. "Oh, my God! Yes! Last night he had the hotel room set up with hundreds and hundreds of wildflowers. They were even in the chandelier! It was absolutely amazing!"

"No roses?"

"No. Everybody does roses. He didn't. I love that he thought so much about it that he knew I'd love the wildflowers. It was like making love in a field somewhere. Can you believe it? He's simply amazing! I've never felt like this before."

Laura tried not to roll her eyes, but she could not control herself. She had heard similar declarations from Sara in the past.

Sara saw Laura's expression and insisted, "Really! This time it's different. I swear."

Laura challenged, "Better than the almighty Joe Lazaro?"

"Yes. I can't even explain how spectacular it was."

Laura held up her hands and laughed. "It's okay. I don't need *all* of the details."

"Well, I'm not giving you *all* the details! I just meant that it was an earth-moving, life-altering experience."

"Well, you've never said *those* words before. So, I guess I have to believe that Phil is the one you've been looking for. Well, at least in bed, he is."

Sara persisted, "He's more than good in bed. Although, he *is* awesome in that department. He is the right man for me, in every way. I know he is. He's in my heart and soul."

"Huh!" Laura embraced Sara. "I'm really glad. You deserve to be happy."

"Thank you. He makes me happier than I've ever been."

The women heard footsteps.

Flora appeared. She greeted Laura and Sara, "Hi!"

Laura and Sara responded, "Hi."

Flora said, "I hope Grandma doesn't get upset. I used the pretty towels in the bathroom, you know, the ones for when company comes. But that's all there was. I didn't know what to do, so I used them."

Laura reassured her, "Don't worry. It's okay. She won't get upset. Once the company is here, it's okay to use them."

Flora replied, "Whew! I wasn't sure."

Laura suggested, "Well, we better get back out there. We wouldn't want to miss any fun."

Flora replied, "I'm having so much fun today. And I'm hungry for the cookies Grandma and I made. There would have been more, but the bad men came and messed everything up."

Sara questioned, "Bad men?"

Animated, Flora said, "Yeah, but Grandma got them good. She hit the one guy with the baking sheet and cookies flew everywhere. It was funny but scary too. Then she hit him with the rolling pin until he stopped moving. Then, I poured oil on the floor and the other one fell. Grandma hit him while I kept throwing stuff at him. He ran out of the house, but Grandma chased after him with her big skillet. She looks funny when she runs." Flora giggled as she imitated Rose running.

Sara and Laura snickered.

Flora resumed, "But he was too fast for her, and he got away. Then Cousin Vinnie came for a visit, and then we had to clean the kitchen."

Skeptical, Laura asked, "Really?"

Pointing at the wall, Flora said, "Yup. See? That dent in the wall is where one guy hit his head."

Confused, the women exchanged glances. They both had thought Flora was making up a story. However, there was a visible dent in the wall.

Flora cheerfully said, "I'm going outside to play now."

Laura said, "Okay."

Sara was closest to the door. So, she opened it.

Flora skipped toward the open door.

CHAPTER 15

WHILE the men played bocce, Spaulding and Sully stood off to the side, near one of the food tables.

Spaulding heard a buzzing sound. He thought, *Too loud for a bug*. He scanned the backyard. Then he looked up and saw a drone carrying a package overhead. "Heads up! Drone."

Ashby and Tony left the bocce area and joined Spaulding and Sully. They watched the drone zigzag across the backyard.

Spaulding drew his firearm and aimed it at the drone.

Sully cautioned, "Don't shoot. We don't know what it is."

Visually tracking the drone, Spaulding stated, "I have a bad feeling about it."

Sully ordered, "Hold."

The drone descended several yards away from the men. It was approximately eight feet off the ground when it dropped the package it carried. The tape used to secure the box failed to keep the box sealed. The cardboard box flaps split open as the box crash-landed.

The men rushed over to it. Other guests were curious, and they approached it as well.

Sully warned, "Everybody, stay back!"

Confused, the guests stopped. However, the team members advanced.

Through the opening, Ashby saw an electronic timer connected to a bomb. He confirmed their worst fear. "Bomb."

Sully shouted, "Bomb! Everybody to the front yard! Go! Go! Go!"

Terrified guests screamed and ran.

CHAPTER 16

SARA heard Sully's warning. She intercepted and scooped up Flora in her arms. She shut the door with her foot. She grabbed Laura's hand and pulled her toward the basement door. She hoped they would be safe in the cellar.

Confused, Flora asked, "A bomb?"

Sara answered, "Don't worry. We're going into the basement to get away from it."

Flora asked, "They're back, aren't they?"

Sara replied, "I don't know. We just need to get to safety."

Holding her lower back with her left hand, Laura complained as they descended, "These stairs are killing me."

Sara encouraged, "You're almost at the bottom. Hang in there."

Flora, Laura, and Sara heard muffled yelling and screaming. Tense and scared, they looked around and up at the ceiling.

Flora yelled, "I knew it! Those bad men are back!"

Sara attempted to sooth Flora, "It's okay. Don't worry. We're going to be okay."

Now, Laura and Sara believed Flora's story. Someone was attacking the house.

Laura cried as she held her stomach. "Not again, God. Not again."

Sara let go of Flora.

Flora stood still, bewildered.

Sara reassured them. "We're going to be fine. Don't worry. Try to stay calm."

Laura choked back a sob. "Easy for you to say. You didn't see what they did last time. I can't go through that again."

Sara racked her brain to understand why someone was targeting the Lazaro family. The robbery Flora described could have been a random event. But, the presence of a bunch of supposed muscular relatives, coupled with a bomb attack, suggested something more personal and sinister.

Finding strength from within, Sara guaranteed, "I'm not going to let anything happen to either of you. I promise."

CHAPTER 17

S PAULDING looked up. The drone still buzzed overhead. He took aim and fired. The bullet hit the camera lens and shattered it. He fired again and hit one of the arm mechanisms that had carried the payload. As he fired a third time, the drone zipped away from the area.

Spaulding scanned the sky for additional threats.

Sully ordered, "Spaulding, go with the family. TJ and White, sweep adjoining yards. Then meet in front of the house. Keep your eyes and ears open! There could be more."

In unison, they replied, "Roger."

As Spaulding, White, and Tony ran their separate ways, Ashby knelt and peeled back the box completely. The timer read two minutes, twenty-six seconds. Ashby swore, "Shit. Dirty bomb."

Synchronizing his watch to the timer, Sully asked, "Can you defuse it?"

Examining the device, Ashby said, "In time? Doubtful. Look at all of these wires. They could be fakes or redundancies or maybe not. I don't know. And I don't have the time to figure it out without my gear or my robot. Go! Save yourself. I'll do what I can."

Stubbornly, Sully refused, "I'm not leaving you."

Flatly, Ashby replied, "No reason for two of us to die today."

Sully called Lee who was offsite doing research. "A dirty bomb was just delivered via a drone. Do you have eyes in the sky?"

Typing quickly, Lee replied, "No. We weren't anticipating a sophisticated strike of any kind."

Sully disconnected the call.

Lee was accustomed to disconnected calls. He quickly searched for traffic cameras and security cameras in the area. If he found anything of value, he would notify the team.

Ashby did not want to sacrifice his own life, but he would, if he had no alternative. Scanning the vicinity, his eyes lit up. He grasped the device gingerly, stood, then broke into a full-run sprint. He shouted, "I've got an idea!"

Sully watched Ashby run toward an in-ground swimming pool in the adjoining neighbor's yard. The Lazaros' backyard was deep, as was the neighbor's yard. He prayed Ashby would reach the pool in time.

TJ and White ran toward Sully. Out of breath, TJ said, "All yards clear."

Sully replied, "Good. Let's hope Ashby's plan works. Get to the front yard."

With fourteen seconds to spare, Ashby threw the bomb into the deep end of the swimming pool and doubled back.

Sully hunkered down behind a large tree. He yelled to Ashby, "Five seconds! Get down!"

Ashby hit the ground, hands protecting his head.

Like a geyser, water and debris shot up and out. The force of the explosion sent a shock wave rippling into the ground. The water and debris that flew high into the air began raining down.

When the hardware hit roofs and pavement, it sounded like large chunks of hail. Many pieces imbedded in the house's siding, tree trunks, the ground, and Ashby's body.

When the metal-laden shower ended, Sully ran to Ashby. He saw shrapnel imbedded in Ashby's back and legs. "Ashby, can you move?

Ashby groaned, "Uh huh. But I'd rather not."

Sully followed up, "How bad?"

Cringing, Ashby replied, "It's not good. But it could have been worse. The water helped absorb some of the energy like I hoped."

Sully complimented, "Quick thinking. Good job. Don't move. Help is on the way."

"Thanks. It was more luck than anything. And do me a favor, tell them to hurry."

CHAPTER 18

U NSURE of what was happening above ground, Sara searched the basement for anything that could be used as a weapon. In one corner, she found an old wrought iron fireplace set. She plucked the poker from the stand.

Flora followed her. "Whatcha doing?"

Good question, kid. Sara decided to tell the truth. "I'm trying to find things to hit the bad guys with."

Flora's eyes widened. "Do I get one?"

Sara offered her the broom. "Is this too heavy for you?"

Flora lifted it. "It is heavy. But I can do it. I *told* Grandma I should work out at the gym to build up my muscles."

Not having time to debate that topic, Sara said, "Okay. Hopefully, we won't need these. It's just in case."

Flora nodded.

Sara handed the shovel to Laura. "It's all I could find."

Sitting on an old lawn chair with frayed green and white fabric, Laura accepted the tool. "If I wasn't so terrified, this would be funny. Us trying to defend ourselves with fireplace tools."

Sara continued to rummage around. Her search yielded a few metal garbage can lids.

Sara handed the lids to Laura and Flora.

Flora asked, "What's this for?"

Instructing her, "We can use them as shields. Grab the handle, and hold it up in front of you."

Lifting it up, Flora asked, "Like this?"

"Yes, good job. But I'm sure that everything will be all right, and we won't have to use them."

Flora nodded. She had confidence in Sara's words. *Grandma and I defeated the bad men before, this lady looks younger and stronger than Grandma. So, we'll beat them again.*

Sara stood at the bottom of the stairs. She was the only one who could realistically fight off an attacker.

As Flora joined Sara at the stairs, they heard a rumble and felt the house shake.

Frightened, Flora screamed.

Putting her arm around Flora, Sara remarked, "The bomb detonated."

Laura muttered, "Oh, my God."

Unsure that her words were the truth, Sara reassured them, "We're okay. We'll be fine down here."

Laura reported, "The baby's kicking really hard." She rubbed her belly in an effort to get the kicking to subside.

Innocently, Flora asked, "Can I feel?"

Laura nodded.

Flora dropped the broom and metal lid and scrambled over to Laura and put her hand flat against Laura's swollen belly. Flora jumped when she felt the baby kick. "Wow! That's so cool! Does it hurt when the baby does that?"

"It doesn't hurt. It's uncomfortable sometimes though."

Pressing her ear to Laura's stomach, she asked, "Is it a girl baby or a boy baby?"

"I don't know yet."

Excitedly, Flora said, "Well, if it's a girl baby, that would be awesome! You could bring her over, and we could play. I could teach her all sorts of stuff. Oh! Important things, like being a princess. I love playing princess. I have lots of princess dresses. I have blue ones, and pink ones, and yellow ones. I'd let her borrow some because I can't wear them all at once."

Laura relaxed a little. "How about if it's a boy?"

Pondering for a moment, Flora answered, "Well ... I could still be a princess. He could be a prince. He's going to need a horse. But Grandma says those are expensive. He could get a pretend horse though."

Sara was grateful Laura had a distraction. It seemed to be calming her down.

As Sara observed Laura interact with Flora, she knew Laura would make a great mother. And Sara felt guilty for previously harboring ill will against this beautiful little girl. *It's not her fault that her mother was a wicked, horrible tramp.*

While feeling grateful for shedding those old feelings, Sara felt her cell phone vibrate in her pocket.

At first, Sara thought having pockets on a maxi dress was weird. However, their present predicament proved their usefulness. The text message was from Phil.

Laura asked, "Who is it? What's going on?"

"It's Phil. He's asking where I am."

Laura said, "Tell him we're down here too."

"Of course, I will." Sara typed, "Basement with Laura and Flora. We're OK. Are you OK?"

He typed back, "I'm A-Okay. Stay put. I'll get you when it's over."

CHAPTER 19

F RANTIC, Joe and Rose shouted as they searched the yard for
Flora. John did the same in his search for Laura.

Phil intercepted them and showed them the text from Sara.

Joe and Rose simultaneously said, "Thank God!"

Joe added, "I don't know what I'd do if anything happened to her."

John silently echoed the sentiment. He could not bear for anything else to happen to his wife and their unborn child.

Phil reassured them, "They're okay. Let's go get them out of the basement."

Sara, Laura, and Flora were still shaken from what felt like an earthquake when they heard commotion above them. All three held the lids in front of themselves as shields.

Sara stood at the bottom of the stairs with the fireplace poker, ready to face an adversary.

Flora's broom was on the ground, next to her.

Laura held the shovel vertically.

None of them spoke as they waited to see what would happen next.

Without warning, the basement door opened.

Sara's mind thought, *Halt! Who goes there?*

However, she yelled, "Stop! We have weapons, and we're not afraid to use them!"

Joe saw Sara holding the shield and poker. "Sara, it's me, Joe."

Relieved, Laura and Sara exhaled sighs of relief and lowered the lids.

Joe bounded down the stairs. "Are you okay?"

Sara nodded.

Flora waved her garbage can lid. "Hi, Daddy! I'm over here. We're ready to beat up the bad men again."

Joe rushed over to her and gave her a bear hug. "Are you okay?"

Pointing at Sara, Flora replied, "Yes. This nice lady picked me up and carried me down here. The house shook. It was weird. Did you feel it? Then I got to feel the pregnant lady's baby kick. Do you want to feel? I'm sure she wouldn't mind. And we have these lids for shields. And I was supposed to use the broom as a sword, but it was too heavy. Grandma was wrong. I really need to build up my muscles at the gym."

Joe's eyes met Sara's. Grateful, he said, "Thank you."

Sara replied, "You're welcome."

John pushed past Sara and rushed over to his wife. "Laura? Are you okay? Is the baby okay?"

She nodded. "Get me up. I have to pee."

John and Sara helped Laura get up out of the lawn chair.

John embraced his wife.

Joe picked up Flora and mounted the stairs.

Laura confessed, "John, I was so afraid. I thought it was happening again."

Leading her up the stairs, John comforted her, "It's over. I've got you now."

Phil waited in the kitchen for Sara to emerge.

A huge smile spread over Sara's face when she saw Phil. His outstretched arms were a sight for sore eyes.

He gave her a bear hug and a kiss. "I'm never going to let you out of my sight again."

Sara laughed. "That could get awkward, you know."

"You know what I mean. Are you okay?"

Sara said, "I do know what you mean. And I'm fine. We were

ready to defend ourselves with fireplace tools and garbage can lids."

"Very resourceful, sweetheart."

"Well, I had a child and a pregnant woman to protect. I had to do something."

He kissed her. "Warrior instincts."

She shrugged. "I guess. What happened out there? We felt the shock wave from the bomb detonating."

Phil reported, "I don't know what's going on. But half the guys here are packing heat. Something's fishy."

"I knew it! I knew something wasn't right when they introduced those people as relatives. They were too stiff, like military guys or cops. Is everyone okay?"

"Looks like everyone is okay except for the guy who took care of the bomb. But to play it on the safe side, I'm getting you out of here."

"Let me find Laura and John, so I can say good-bye. I don't plan on coming back here for a long, long time, if ever."

Before Sara could search for her friends, Joe intercepted her.

Joe asked, "Can we talk for a minute?"

She answered, "Yes."

Realizing a conversation between the former lovers was necessary, Phil said, "I'll be outside if you need me."

Sara said, "Thank you. I'll be out in a few minutes."

Confident, Phil kissed her on the cheek. "Take whatever time you need."

She nodded.

After Phil left the kitchen, Joe said, "I want to thank you again for taking care of Flora like you did."

Sara shrugged. "It was nothing."

Joe said, "It wasn't nothing. You protected her despite how you feel about her."

"It's not really her. She's cute. It's more about her crazy slut of a mother."

Shifting uneasily from foot to foot, Joe said, "Yeah. I get that."

Sara leaned against the kitchen counter. "So?"

Uncomfortable, Joe said, "Um, you look good."

On an adrenaline high from the excitement, Sara replied, "I am good."

Although Joe wanted to hold her, kiss her, and have everything revert back to the way it used to be, Sara's body language told him it was not a possibility. He said, "That's good."

Sara was amazed and relieved that she did not feel the usual sexual attraction toward him. Instead, she pitied him. The exchanges of "good" back and forth were awkward and forced.

She asked, "Was there something else you wanted to say?"

Knowing he had nothing left to lose, Joe confessed, "I still love you, Sara. I just wanted you to know. I'd do absolutely anything to get you back. Anything at all. You know that Mita's dead. So, you'll never have to deal with her. And I know you'll come to love Flora. She's a great kid."

Seeing the desperation in his eyes, Sara replied, "I know. Flora is adorable. But I'm sorry. I don't feel the same way. I'm with Phil now. I've moved on. It's time you moved on too."

Joe answered, "I've loved you for so long. I don't know if I can."

Sara pointed out, "You've been with plenty of other women over the years."

He declared, "I always compared them to you. No one ever measured up."

Sara understood. She had done the same thing. Until Phil. Phil changed everything.

Sara said, "Our lives are going in different directions. I'm focusing on my photography. Phil and I are going to start a foundation together to help preserve the National Parks."

Each time she told someone the plan, it seemed more and more of a reality and less of a dream.

Joe remarked, "I had no idea. I knew you liked taking pictures, and hiking, and stuff. But working to preserve parks? I never would have guessed. Are you sure it's what you want to do?"

"Yes. It is. I've thought long and hard about it. I can't work in a cubical and live a life where I'm just looking forward to retirement. Corporate America is not for me. It never was. I want to live my life now, not put it on hold until I'm too old to do half of the things I want to do."

"Huh. I guess you have thought about it."

"I haven't just thought about it. I'm doing it. I already have a large catalog of pictures to work with."

"I wouldn't stop you from doing that."

She continued, "Yes, you would. You'd want me here. But I'm not going to stay here. I'll be travelling all the time. You couldn't travel with me. You have Flora to think about. I could never be a mother to her. She's a constant reminder of what you did. You need to concentrate on being a good father to her."

"I am. That's all I've been doing since you left."

"With a lot of unsolicited advice from your mother, I'm sure."

"Yeah. But she's been great with her. I was just hoping ..."

"I'm sorry. But you'll find someone else. Your mom will make sure of it."

Joe pleaded, "But we're supposed to be together. I just need one more chance to prove it to you. It's our destiny. You've said so yourself. We've been through so much. We're destined to be together."

"I used to think that. But everything has changed. Think about everything I just told you. About preserving the parks. About my new mindset, goals, and travelling. I mean, *everything*. I really am sorry, Joe. We're not destined to be together. My future is going in a completely different direction. And I couldn't be happier about it. I know that's not what you want to hear. But it's the truth."

Joe poured out his heart, "But I love you, Sara. I've never loved anyone as much as I've loved you. I can't live without you."

"I'm sorry, Joe. I'm not in love with you anymore. I don't know what else to say. I'm sorry."

Dejected, he said, "I guess this is it then."

Sympathetic, she answered, "Yes, Joe. It is. You know you will always have a special place in my heart."

Tears ran down Joe's cheeks. His heart was breaking again. "Uh huh. You know the same goes for me. I will always love you, Sara."

Sara hugged her former lover. "I know. Take care of yourself, Joe."

He hugged her back, knowing it would probably be the last time he held her in his arms. "You too. Be happy."

"You too, Joe."

Phil watched the former lovers' exchange through the window.

Rose walked up and joined Phil. "So, what do you think they're talking about?"

Matter-of-factly, Phil replied, "She's telling him that it's over for them."

"You think so, do you?"

Crossing his arms, he said, "Not to be rude, ma'am, but yes. Your son took her for granted. He didn't appreciate her or treasure her as I do. If he had, things might have worked out differently. But he couldn't keep it in his pants. So, here we are."

Rose scoffed. "Huh! Well, that was years ago. They have a long history."

Phil challenged, "I know all about their history. And that's exactly what it is—history. He was part of her past. I'm her present and future."

With eyebrows raised, Rose asked, "Pretty confident, aren't you?"

Smiling, he answered, "Yes, I am. Helping her achieve the goals she has set for herself and making sure she is happy overall are the most important things to me. Period."

Unconvinced, Rose said, "We'll see."

He chuckled. He knew what she meant by that comment. "I can tell you're a ballbuster, Rose. But you don't intimidate me. I'm sure of myself, of Sara, and our future."

"Huh!"

Phil continued, "You can argue and protest all you want. But you need to accept reality. This is out of your control. She's made her decision. You and your son need to deal with it."

Rose crossed her arms and pursed her lips.

Cognizant he was irritating her, he said, "I know you're used to getting your own way, hell or high water. But this time, you're not going to win."

Sara approached them. She asked, "Have you seen Laura?"

Rose replied, "She and John left."

"Sorry I missed them. Oh well. I'll call her tomorrow to check on her." Turning to Phil, she asked, "Ready to go?"

Phil answered, "Yes." Addressing Rose, he said, "Good evening, ma'am."

Sara said, "Good night, Mrs. Lazaro."

Rose responded, "Good night."

Rose watched them leave. As much as she wanted Sara for her son, Joe, she knew that ship had indeed sailed. And she knew that even her best chocolate cake would provide little comfort to her broken-hearted son.

CHAPTER 20

POLICE had cordoned off the block surrounding the Lazaro home. The utility companies sent crews out to check for leaks in the gas and water lines. Neighbors congregated on the sidewalks. They huddled in small groups, trying to catch a glimpse of something.

Paramedics who were at the party assessed Ashby's injuries and tended to his wounds until the ambulance arrived. The shrapnel injuries he sustained were located on his back and legs. So, he was strapped to the board face down and transported to the hospital.

John insisted Laura go to the hospital and get checked by a doctor. All the other guests were cleared by the police.

Phil and Sara ducked under the crime scene tape. While Phil attempted to figure out what street address to give to the car service for a ride, he and Sara were approached by a young man.

The young man said, "Excuse me, I'm Adam Blue, a reporter for the daily paper. I was wondering if you could tell me what happened."

Sara answered, "I was in the house. Someone yelled, 'Bomb!' I ran into the basement and waited. I didn't see anything." Pointing to Phil, she said, "But he was outside."

Turning his attention to Phil, he asked, "Can you tell me what happened?"

Phil conveyed, "Like she said, I heard someone yell, 'Bomb!' We were told to run to the front of the house. It was chaos after that. But some guy threw the bomb in a swimming pool. He was hit by some projectiles, but everyone else is fine."

He inquired, "So, just that one guy was injured?"

Phil replied, "Yes."

"Are either of you related to the people who own the house?"

Sara answered, "No. Neither of us are. Just friends of the family. We were there for the party for our other friends."

Appearing distracted, he said, "Oh, okay."

Sara asked, "Aren't you going to record us or write anything down?"

The reporter muttered, "I've got it on my phone."

Sara and Phil exchanged confused looks. The man was not holding a phone in either hand.

Sara asked, "Anything else?"

The young man said, "No."

Phil took Sara's hand in his as they walked away from the reporter.

Phil stated, "Something was off about that guy."

Sara agreed, "You're right. He didn't write anything down or record us. And come to think of it, he didn't ask our names. What reporter doesn't ask for the names of witnesses?"

Phil turned around. The reporter was nowhere in sight.

Sara said, "We'd better say something."

Reluctantly, they headed back toward the house.

CHAPTER 21

AS Sara and Phil relayed the encounter with the supposed reporter to Vinnie, Tony joined them.

Vinnie asked, "Do you think you would recognize him if you saw him again?"

Sara and Phil nodded affirmatively.

Tony said, "Hang tight. We'll get some pictures for you to look at."

Sara questioned, "We? Are you trying out law enforcement now, Tony?"

Rose revealed, "My Anthony has been undercover for years. We just found out."

Tony yelled, "Ma!"

Rose replied, "What? I didn't realize you were still trying to keep that a secret. Seems like half the town already knows."

Flabbergasted, Sara stated, "I must be on an episode of *The Twilight Zone.*"

Rose quipped, "Welcome to my world."

Attempting to wrap her head around the news, Sara asked, "You're really a cop?"

Rose corrected, "He's an undercover government agent."

Sara asked, "So the pizza franchise thing?"

Tony replied, "A cover story. Like all the other ideas."

Stunned, Sara sat down. "Wow! I never saw that coming. No offense, but you're the last person I ever would have guessed to be in law enforcement."

"No offense taken. It was part of my job to throw everyone off the trail."

"Kudos to you on that front."

Lee had arrived just before Sara and Phil reentered the house. He pulled his laptop out of his bag and entered his password. "It will just take a minute or two to pull up some pictures for you to look at."

Trying to lighten the mood, Phil joked, "Is it usually this crazy around here?"

Sara rolled her eyes. "Yes, but there's always cake or brownies. So, that makes everything better."

Vinnie smirked and shook his head. He had to admit there was some truth in her words. His Aunt Rose's cakes and brownies were delicious.

Lee handed Sara his computer. "Here are some photos."

The pictures were all known associates and male relatives of Al Fuentes.

Vinnie instructed, "Let us know if you recognize any of them."

Still reeling from the revelation that Tony was a government agent, Sara scanned the images.

While Sara perused the pictures, Phil asked Tony, "These guys aren't all relatives from California, are they? Sara said she didn't recognize any of them."

Tony admitted, "No. They're not. They're members of my task force."

Phil questioned, "So, you knew something was going to happen?"

Running his fingers through his thinning hair, Tony replied, "Not for sure, we didn't."

Crossing his arms, Phil asked, "Who's the target?"

Tony stated, "Everybody living in this house."

Fishing, Phil asked, "Why?"

Tony answered, "It's complicated and classified."

Phil replied, "I'd say so. It's complicated and serious enough that whoever they are, they tried to bomb your house."

"The less you know, the better off you are."

Scrolling through the pictures, Sara said, "I beg to differ. We could have died."

Phil noted, "From the looks of her, your mother seems more distraught over the neighbor's house and pool than anything. I don't understand you people at all."

Tony replied, "Don't let her fool you. She's upset about everything. But she feels guilty about the house and pool because they were damaged because of us."

Phil stated, "But the alternative was that people could have been killed."

"Obviously, neither scenario was good. But she knows that Ashby will be okay. And she knows no one else was hurt. So, she's shifted gears to worrying about the neighbors."

"Huh."

Shrugging, Tony continued, "She'll bake a cake for Ashby for his heroics and another one for the neighbors to soften the blow."

Shaking his head, Phil said, "This is absurd. I don't get it. What is it about this woman and her cakes?"

Looking up from the laptop, Sara attested, "They're really, really good."

Phil teased, "Lose-your-mind, orgasm good?"

Sara replied, "If you asked me two days ago, I would have said, 'Yes.' But after what you and I shared last night, I'd have to say, 'No.'"

Shuddering, Tony complained, "Come on! I didn't need to hear that."

Sara laughed. "I'd apologize, but I'm not sorry."

Phil appeared to stand taller as he waited for his turn on the computer.

Tony chided, "Can you focus on the pictures, please?"

After another minute, Sara pointed to one of the photos. She exclaimed, "That's him!"

Lee asked, "You're sure?"

"I'm positive."

Lee relieved Sara of the computer, reset the photo order, and handed the laptop to Phil. "Okay. Now your turn."

After several minutes, Phil identified the same man. "This is him."

Pleased, Lee said, "Okay. Great! You both identified the same guy—Marco Moreno."

Phil asked, "Who's he?"

Typing, Lee replied, "He's looking like our ringleader."

Phil inquired, "Ringleader for what?"

Tony said, "It's classified."

Sara piped up, "We could have been killed. I think we have the right to know what's going on."

Tony remained tightlipped.

Lee buried his head in his laptop and avoided eye contact.

Rose answered, "Some crazy people have a vendetta against our family. They're trying to kill us."

Flabbergasted, Sara asked, "What? Why?"

Rose simplified the situation. "Anthony got mixed up with the wrong people."

Sara questioned, "Like who? Drug dealers?"

"No. These degenerates are trying to get even because some family members died during Anthony's last case. If they can't get to Anthony, they'll settle for us."

Tony warned, "Ma, you're not supposed to say anything."

Annoyed, Rose said, "Right. Because keeping it a secret has kept us so safe. Give me a break. At this point, does it really matter? I think if we get the word out, we could catch them quicker. Come to think of it, we should start up the neighborhood watch again."

Tony sighed.

Sara asked, "Are the people who attacked today the same people from the church massacre?"

Rose replied, "Looks like it."

Agitated, Sara said, "Oh, my God! And you had a party here knowing that? Knowing you were targets, and they could attack any time?"

Rose stated, "We didn't expect them to try anything like this."

Furious, Sara scolded, "What did you expect? They attacked in broad daylight in front of a church. A *church* wasn't safe. You think a backyard party is immune? You put *everyone* in danger unnecessarily. Don't you think Laura's been through enough? She's pregnant. She could have lost the baby because you were too stubborn to cancel a damn party or let someone else host it."

Rose crossed her arms. Sternly, she asked, "Are you about done?"

Standing up to Rose, Sara replied, "No. Not by a long shot. Do you understand what you've done? Laura's a mess. John's a mess. If something happens to their baby, it's on all of you. I expect more from you, Mrs. Lazaro! You pride yourself on being a protector. Instead, you're putting everyone you're in contact with in danger. Can't you see that?"

"Now, listen ..."

Sara interrupted, "No, you're the one who needs to listen. You never think of anyone except yourself. You always claim you're doing it for the good of this one or that one. You dominate everyone around you and their relationships. You always have to get your way, and at what cost?"

"*Now*, are you done?"

Feeling the power rise within her, Sara proclaimed, "No. I don't mean to be disrespectful, Mrs. Lazaro. You have been kind to me. But your constant interference has hurt more than it has helped."

Rose tapped her foot impatiently waiting for Sara to finish.

Sara gestured widely. "Look around. You had to take over and be in charge. You had to control everything. Look how that turned out. How many more people need to get hurt or die for you to wake up? You somehow think you can conquer these people by ignoring them? It's time you got your head out of the sand. You're not protecting anyone. You're doing the exact opposite. You're going to get someone you love killed. Then, how will you feel? How will you feel when there's even more blood on your hands?"

No one had ever spoken that way to Rose. There was dead

silence. No one dared to even breathe while waiting for the tirade which would most likely follow.

Rose walked over to Sara.

The room was completely silent. No one moved.

Their faces were mere inches apart.

Sara was steady and held firm.

Rose said, "You know that everything I do, I do for my family. I will protect them at all costs. I agree that I have failed them lately. And I plan to remedy that immediately."

Stunned, everyone breathed a collective sigh of relief.

Turning to Sully, Rose said, "You need to give me options."

Surprised, Sully nodded. "We can do that."

Rose addressed Sara, "Congratulations, dear. You've finally found your voice. Impressive. And it's about damn time."

CHAPTER 22

MARCO seethed as he drove Jenny's red Mazda Miata home. He had borrowed it since his car would attract too much unwanted attention. He knew he could not risk getting his window fixed. The police would have notified the body shops and glass replacement companies of the car's involvement in a crime.

He had told Jenny that he was having his car's windows re-tinted because there were air bubbles between the window and the original tint. She believed him.

Sparkling pink strands of beads hung from the rearview mirror. The steering wheel and seats were wrapped in fuzzy pink covers. Astounded at Jenny's horrendous taste in car accessories, he remarked, "At least the exterior paint job of this thing isn't pink."

Marco wanted to blame the early package release on a mechanical malfunction. However, he could not. He saw the gun aimed at the drone. His impatience and fear of failure triggered the early release. As a result, that caused the detonation timing to be off and allowed someone to be a hero.

For the second time, his plans had been thwarted. The Lazaros were unscathed. His drone's camera was destroyed. Two arms were damaged. He hoped there was no additional damage to the equipment, but he would have to take it apart to find out.

Marco pulled into Jenny's assigned space in the parking garage. Then he removed the wounded drone from the car and carried it into the apartment.

He deposited the drone in his office. Then, he turned on the computer monitor to watch the little dots float on the map in front of him. He loved how people failed to disable their GPS locators.

I need to refine my plan, or else, I won't accomplish my objective. I'll use the GPS information again to track their movements. Although, next time, I'm convinced I'll succeed.

In the meantime, Marco needed to work off his excess energy. "Jenny! Where are you?"

Calling out from the bedroom, she answered, "In here."

She's always in the bedroom. Nice to know I can count on something.

Marco entered the bedroom and was excited to see a variety of sex toys and leather straps on the bed and dresser.

Jenny cracked a whip in his direction. "I went shopping yesterday. I thought we could try out some new playthings today."

He commented, "You must have read my mind. I have a lot of energy to burn."

In a low, sultry voice, she replied, "Excellent. And I guarantee you'll be satisfied as long as you do what you're told."

Shedding his clothes, he asked, "If I'm not satisfied, then what do I get to do to you?"

Exuding confidence, she answered, "It won't come to that. And if you do exactly everything you're told, as a reward, I'll allow you to do that special thing you love to do with the hot wax."

Eagerly, he pledged, "I will do absolutely anything as long as hot wax is my ultimate reward."

Cracking the whip in his direction again, she said, "Good. Let's begin."

CHAPTER 23

VINNIE announced, "The forensics team is still processing the backyard. They're thorough, but you'll probably find bolts and screws in the trees and yard for some time."

Rose said, "Wonderful."

Vinnie continued, "The pool is a total loss, but there was just minor damage to the back of the house. Good thing they weren't home at the time. The gas company confirmed there were no leaks. But two water lines were damaged."

Sal commented, "It could have been worse."

Vinnie agreed, "Yes, it could have been."

Sully reported, "Ashby's having surgery to remove all of the metal fragments. He was lucky. Nothing hit a major artery or vein."

Vinnie added, "And John said that Laura and the baby are okay. There weren't any other reports of injuries. So, everyone's fine."

Sara said, "That's all good news."

Disgusted, Rose replied, "Fine? You think everyone is fine? Traumatized is more like it."

Vinnie said, "I just meant ..."

Tony interrupted, "We know what you meant. Thanks for the update."

Sully said, "If Moreno is sophisticated and tech savvy enough to drop a dirty bomb via a drone, we must assume he's tracking your phones, and possibly, your vehicles."

Sal said, "Geez. How do we stop him from doing that?"

Sully replied, "For the time being, we don't."

Rose questioned, "Why? Are you crazy?"

Sully answered, "No. We don't want to tip him off. This way he still thinks he has the upper hand."

Exasperated, Rose threw up her hands. "But he does! This is ridiculous."

Flora colored a picture at the kitchen table. She tuned out the arguing around her by humming a song in her head. This situation reminded her of when her mother used to yell and scream at her.

Joe stayed with Flora, while the rest of the adults argued in the family room. It was easier to sit with Flora than watch Sara with Phil.

Rose stated, "I don't want to be separated from my family. But we need to do something. What options do we have?"

Sully replied, "The ever-unpopular solution in your eyes—disappear, and go into protective custody. We can protect you."

Rose balked, "Forgive me if I don't have a great deal of confidence in your abilities at the moment."

Sully bristled. "We didn't realize they'd be sophisticated enough to use drones. Nothing in that family's history indicated they would use that type of technology. We underestimated them. And that was our fault. However, we will be changing our strategy to combat this new threat."

Unconvinced, Rose uttered, "Uh huh."

Phil piped up, "I have an idea that I know will work."

Irritated, Rose questioned, "Why are you still even here?"

Sara answered for the both of them. "We weren't sure if Vinnie had any more questions about our run-in with that Marco Moreno guy. So, we figured we'd hang around until he told us we could go."

Vinnie said, "I think we're good. You can go if you want to."

Despite their limited interaction playing bocce, Sal had sized up Phil as a resourceful guy. And resourceful guys often have good ideas. Sal interjected, "Let's hear his idea first. It's not like it can hurt."

Indignant, Rose asked, "What? He's an outsider and doesn't know anything about our family. How can he help?"

Sal justified, "That's precisely why I think he might be able to help. He has fresh eyes. He has no bias." He turned to Phil. "The floor is yours."

Phil acknowledged, "Thanks."

Overruled, Rose said, "Fine, let's hear it."

Phil said, "I'd call it, 'Operation Subterfuge.' And it will solve all of your problems for the time being."

Rose stated, "That's highly doubtful."

Phil said, "You haven't even heard what I have to say yet."

Patting his leg, Sara explained, "You just have to get used to her."

Phil replied, "I don't plan on staying long enough for that to happen."

Sal scolded, "Enough from the peanut gallery. Let him talk."

Phil suggested, "One of my relatives has a house for sale in the mountains. There's one road in and out. Easy to see when someone is coming. It's on ten acres. It's secluded. So, there won't be any nosy neighbors. It would be easy to install a security system with cameras around the perimeter. It's heavily-wooded, so I don't think drones would be an issue. It's completely off the grid. And none of you have ties to the area."

Sully nodded as he considered the merits of the idea.

Without considering input from anyone else, Rose declined, "That's generous, but no, thank you."

Sully said, "I'd like to hear the rest."

Ignoring Rose, Phil resumed, "I've also got a guy who has a lot of old cars. No GPS in any of them. He can hook you up with loaners. You ditch your phones and anything else that can be used to track you. You drive yourselves there in the old cars undetected."

Rose shook her head.

Phil continued, "There's plenty of room for all of you to be together. You'll be safe. No one would think of looking for you there. And you're not half a world away from the rest of your family."

Sully commented, "It's workable."

Playing devil's advocate, Rose asked, "And how are we supposed to not be seen getting into these cars? You said he's watching us at all times. It won't work, plain and simple."

Sara suggested, "Wait. How about the mall?"

Rose questioned, "What about the mall?"

Excitedly, Sara replied, "It has underground parking. You all go to the mall and switch cars in the underground garage."

Sully agreed, "That would work."

Phil said, "My guy can have the cars there waiting for you. It's a perfect plan."

Sara smiled. She was proud of their ingenuity to develop the plan together, on the spot.

Suspicious, Rose asked, "Why would you do this for us?"

Justifying his offer, Phil said, "You need a place off the grid. The car swap is the only way to get you out of town unnoticed. And there's a vacant house that's not being used. So, why not?"

Still not satisfied, Rose asked, "What's in this for you?"

Exasperated, he replied, "Nothing other than offering a helping hand. I'm just trying to be nice."

Rose harrumphed.

Supporting the plan, Tony said, "You know, it *would* work."

Rose commented, "We'll see."

Phil said, "Whatever. It's late. Sara and I are going to the hotel. We'll be flying out tomorrow morning."

Tony shook Phil's hand. "Thanks for the idea and the offer."

Phil said, "I'm a problem solver, and I have access to resources. This problem had a fairly easy solution. I'll contact my friend and let him know you might be contacting him. I'll text you his number. And I'll give my cousin a heads-up about having some temporary guests. You really should take me up on my offer."

Sully declared, "I like it. The only sticking point is no existing security system. But we've installed systems on the fly before. We can install it once we arrive. Otherwise, it's a sound plan."

Tony agreed, "Okay. It's settled then. Let's hammer out the details."

Unhappy that her objections were ignored, Rose said, "I'll go make some coffee."

CHAPTER 24

O N the ride to the hotel, Sara said, "That was very generous of
you."

Phil replied, "I was just trying to help. I don't think Rose is
going to take help from me though. And that's fine. On second
thought, I don't think the mountain is big enough for the both of
us anyway."

Sara laughed. "You're probably right. She'd end up ruining the
peacefulness and tranquility you've fought so hard to preserve."

Shaking his head, he said, "I swear, I don't know how you put
up with that three-ring circus for so many years."

She shrugged. "Eh. You get used to it."

Phil disagreed, "I would never get used to that. Way too much
drama. I mean, even without the bomb attack, there was too much
drama."

"I guess."

He exclaimed, "And good God, there's Rose! I can't imagine
dealing with her and battling against her constantly. It would be
the most frustrating and maddening thing I can think of. And
doing that day-in and day-out? No way. What a headache."

Sara explained, "Most of the time, everyone lets her have her
way. It's easier."

"That's no way to live. What a nightmare."

Snuggling against him, she said, "A nightmare I escaped from."

He kissed her nose. "I originally intended for this evening to
end a bit differently."

She agreed, "Yes, me too. But I can't get today's events off my mind. I just keep thinking about the danger we were all in. We could have been severely injured or killed."

He squeezed her. "It does make you stop and think and appreciate life a little bit more."

"Yes, it does. And I promise, I'll never take you or what we have together for granted. I'm really lucky to have you."

"I'm the lucky one, sweetheart."

"But I can't help worrying about the rest of them. Granted, they have driven me crazy for years, but I don't want to see any of them dead. I can't imagine what they're going through, living with that level of stress and fear. I mean, can you imagine always wondering if someone was going to attack or kill you? I think I'd go nuts."

"Yeah, that would be an incredible amount of stress. Hopefully, they'll catch the guys soon, and it will all be over."

"I sure hope so."

CHAPTER 25

FROM Rose's family room couch, Sully stated, "Well, Marco Moreno demonstrated his intentions loud and clear today."

Spaulding commented, "And we have to find him before he decides to drop another bomb on the house."

Sully asked, "Do we have anything on his car yet?"

Lee said, "No. The Department of Motor Vehicle's entire site is down for an upgrade to a new system. I can't access the old or new system. The major car dealers have antiquated systems and many of the independent dealers don't have any online sales data. But I'm still trying to find that needle in the haystack."

Switching gears, Sully asked, "Do we have anything on the drone?"

Lee said, "No. We weren't monitoring airspace. Nothing indicated we needed to. Did anyone get a good look at it?"

Spaulding responded, "It wasn't as big as the military-grade drones I've seen. It had a camera, that I shot and disabled. And it had been fitted with equipment to carry and release a payload."

Lee said, "Military-grade drones usually operate at a higher altitude, above five hundred feet. And they're hard to get if you're a civilian. My guess is that it's a modified version of one of the higher end commercial drones that you can buy around town. Thousands of drones have been purchased within sixty miles of Clear Brook. But I know someone who might be able to help in the drone department."

Sully ordered, "Okay. Lee, use whatever resources you can to track down the drone. Dive deep, and get me everything you can find on Marco Moreno. In the meantime, I'm going to pay Carlo Fuentes, Al's brother, a visit. White, you come with me."

White confirmed by nodding.

Tony said, "Hold up a minute."

Sully asked, "Yes?"

Tony suggested, "Since Ma isn't keen on going to the Adirondacks, I was thinking that we should use my safe house instead. It's a lot closer. It already has a security system and a cache of weapons. We can still use the cars without GPS to drive there."

Sully replied, "That's fine by me. Less for us to have to do. Is it big enough to house your family though?"

Tony admitted, "It will be tight, but they'll fit. Hopefully, it will only be for a short time."

"It's your family. If your mother complains to me about the accommodations, I'll be deferring to you."

"Understood. I'll let her know."

Half-jokingly, Sully said, "We'll stay in here, where it's safe."

Tony joined his mother in the kitchen. "Ma, we made a decision we think you're going to like."

With a disbelieving look, Rose asked, "You think so?"

"Yes. We're going to my safe house instead of the house Phil was talking about in the mountains. It's closer and already has a security system."

Handing him a tray of coffee mugs, Rose said, "Good. Take these in there before the coffee gets cold."

Tony accepted the tray and carried it to the other room. Placing the tray on the coffee table in front of his teammates, he said, "Ma okayed going to my safe house."

Sully selected a mug. "That makes things easier all the way around."

Tony agreed, "Yup."

Sully said, "Spaulding, you stay here at the house with TJ and the family. White, you're with me. Lee, you can work from wherever it makes sense."

Lee inserted his earbuds. "I'm good anywhere, as long as I have my music."

Encouraged by the agreement for the new plan, Sully said, "You have your assignments. Let's go catch ourselves some bad guys."

CHAPTER 26

S ULLY and White stood on Carlo Fuentes' front porch. Sully rang the bell.

Opening the door, Carlo asked, "Can I help you?"

Flashing an FBI badge, Sully replied, "We're hoping you can. This is about the vendetta your family has against a government agent."

Carlos denied, "I don't know what you're talking about."

Sully insisted, "You know you do."

Carlo responded, "Let's say I do. Why would I want to help you after what law enforcement has done to my family? Do you know how many funerals I've attended in the past year?"

White said, "We're trying to stop that from happening. You're the head of your family now. We're hoping you can talk some sense into whoever is doing this."

"I don't know what you're talking about."

Sully said, "Play dumb if you want to. But hear this, your cousin, Marco Moreno, sent his brothers to kill an agent and his family. When they failed, he decided to drop a dirty bomb in a suburban neighborhood this afternoon."

Startled, Carlo said, "A bomb? A dirty bomb? You're lying."

Sully responded, "I wish I was lying. He planned an attack today during a backyard party for a pregnant woman and her husband."

Carlo was stunned. He knew the Moreno boys had taken their father's death hard. But he had no idea that they would seek out revenge to this extent.

White asked, "How much more bloodshed does there have to be until you get involved?"

Carlo stood silently.

Sully fished, "Unless you're already involved?"

Carlo replied, "I am *not* involved. How many people were hurt?"

White informed him, "Due to the quick thinking of one agent, he was the only one injured while disposing of the bomb."

Carlo exhaled sharply.

Sully urged, "You need to convince Marco to turn himself in. They'll be adding him to the terrorist watchlist now. You can't just go around dropping dirty bombs in America and expect to get away with it. Turning himself in is his best bet. Every agency will be after him. They'll shoot first and ask questions later. You know that's how it's going to go. It won't end well for him if he forces them to hunt him down."

Shaking his head in dismay, Carlo pledged, "I'll see what I can do."

Sully replied, "Yeah, you do that."

CHAPTER 27

S TIR-CRAZY, Tony paced back and forth on the family room carpet.

Rose complained, "You're going to ruin my carpet. If you want to be useful, you could vacuum."

Without answering, Tony walked out of the room and into the kitchen.

Sal was peering into the refrigerator.

Tony complained, "That's her answer to everything—cleaning. Well, that and food."

Sal replied, "Good food does solve a lot of problems."

"I'm being serious, Dad."

"So am I, Anthony. Have you ever wondered why the answers are always cleaning or food-related?"

"No. I never really thought about it."

Pulling out a chair, Sal offered, "Sit. Let me educate you."

Tony sat.

Sal joined him at the table. "Take cleaning for instance. On the surface, dirt seems to be the problem. Cleaning is the solution. It's within her control to fix that particular problem. When you or your brother have a problem that she can't fix, she turns to cleaning as a substitute. Now, if everything is already clean, or especially if she perceives you need comfort, consoling, or love, then she turns to cooking and baking. Cooking and baking are expressions of love. *Capisce?*"

It dawned on him. "It's how she copes."

"Exactly. Now you understand why she does what she does."

"Yes, I do. Thanks."

"Don't mention it."

Sensing an end to their conversation, Lee said, "TJ, you aren't going to believe this."

Tony asked, "What?"

Excited, Lee reported, "Marco Moreno is one of the people working on the drone system that delivery companies want to use to deliver packages right to your door. And coincidentally, he is in possession of one of the prototype drones from the company's fleet."

Tony exclaimed, "Perfect! Then they have a way to track it."

Lee replied, "Yes and no. He's a sophisticated programmer. He's reprogrammed the device, and he's bouncing his location all over the world."

"Is it hopeless?"

"Not completely. The company is working with me to locate their drone. They're hoping they can hack it and reinitialize the device. They want their expensive prototype back."

"Good."

Lee continued, "I've arranged to meet their top programmer. He's agreed to be part of the team to apprehend Marco and retrieve the drone."

"That's fantastic."

"I just notified Sully. He was pretty stoked about it."

Tony had a hard time picturing Sully being stoked about anything. He asked, "Does the company have a home address for Moreno?"

"No. The address he gave them is a Post Office box. And he didn't spend any of his free time hanging out with anyone at the company. No one knows where he lives."

<h1 style="text-align:center">CHAPTER 28</h1>

CARLO Fuentes made a few phone calls and tracked down his cousin, Marco Moreno, at his girlfriend's apartment. Carlo waited for Jenny to leave before approaching the unit.

When Marco opened the door, Carlo pushed past him.

Sarcastically, Marco said, "Great to see you, cuz. Why don't you come in?"

Carlo waited for Marco to shut the door.

Facetiously, Marco asked, "And to what do I owe the pleasure of your company?"

Getting right to the point, Carlo answered, "You must stop this vendetta."

Nonchalantly, Marco replied, "I don't know what you're talking about."

Getting in Marco's face, Carlo persisted, "You're playing with fire. First, you engineer and botch a murder plot that landed your brother, Nico, in the hospital. He'll end up in jail after the doctors check him out. And as soon as the cops find Lou, he'll join him."

Marco said, "If they know what's good for them, they'll keep their mouths shut."

"You don't get it. Today's dirty bomb stunt was an act of terrorism. Do you understand what you've done? You've gotten yourself on the terrorist watchlist."

"Huh?"

Carlo reiterated, "You are a *terrorist*, like those ISIS assholes on television. Everyone from the local police, FBI, ATF, and Homeland are looking for your sorry ass. You dropped a dirty bomb in a suburban neighborhood. What the hell were you thinking? You're lucky no one got killed. You're going to end up locked away for a long time. And for what?"

Arrogantly, Marco answered, "Justice."

Carlo challenged, "Justice? You don't understand this type of justice. Your father and I grew up in a kill-or-be-killed world. You, and your brothers, and your cousins didn't. My generation made sure that your generation would be out of the family business and the old ways."

Marco said, "They were the good ways."

Carlo disagreed, "No, they weren't. They were not the good old days. Your father knew what he was doing. He knew the risks. You were not born into the same type of life. None of you were."

Marco scoffed.

Carlo grabbed him by the shirt. "You want to live by the old ways and rules? Fine. I'm guessing you've never been in a fist fight, let alone a knife fight or a gun fight. So, by old school rules, you're a coward."

"No, I'm not."

Carlo explained, "Real men fight one-on-one. We look our enemies in the eyes. We might have done some unforgiveable things in our lives, but never, ever would we have considered dropping a dirty bomb where women and children were present. Bombs are for cowards. You're a nobody. You're not even a man."

Indignant, Marco responded, "Yes, I am! I'm going to be a hero. I'll be the patriarch of the family."

Carlo pushed Marco against the wall. "Not even close, you stupid kid. You haven't paid your dues. You don't have any battle scars. You're weak. No one will recognize you as the head of anything. And if you don't turn yourself in, all you'll be when the cops are done with you is dead."

Marco squirmed to get Carlo to release him. "You're wrong."

Carlo refused to release him. Speaking slowly, firmly, Carlo said, "You keep telling yourself that. But you've proven you're nothing. You keep failing. Do you understand what a disgrace you are?"

Still defiant, Marco said, "You're wrong, old man."

Carlo laughed. "Old man? Well, kid, this old man has you pinned to a wall in your own apartment. I could kill you in an instant, and no one would be the wiser."

Fear crossed Marco's eyes. "But you wouldn't. My mother ..."

"But I could." He paused for effect. "And to bring your mother up during an exchange like this just goes to prove what a punk you are."

Disgusted, Carlo walked away.

Marco straightened his wrinkled T-shirt.

"If your father had allowed you to be in the family business, he would be so disappointed in you. I know I am. You're a complete disgrace. You need to man-up."

Marco spat at his cousin.

That act of disrespect enraged Carlo. The veins in his neck popped as his face reddened.

Marco scrambled to get away. But Carlo grabbed and yanked his arm.

Marco whined, "Ow!"

"Ow? Are you kidding me? Some big man you are, whining like a little girl. Are you going to cry now? Huh?"

Marco remained silent as he winced.

Carlo shook his head. "Your father didn't want this for you. He made sure you got the best education money could buy, so you would not follow in his footsteps. But here you are."

With false bravado, Marco said, "What can I say? I am my father's son."

"No, you're not. Like I said, Marco, you are a coward. Disgracing him. Disgracing the entire family."

Marco shook himself free. "No, I'm not. You'll see. I'll prove you wrong. I'm going to be a hero. The family is going to be proud of me."

"Proud of you? You've gotten yourself classified as a terrorist.

Terrorists aren't heroes. You're an enemy of the whole fucking country. Do you understand? You're on the terrorist watchlist. That means you have a target painted on you. Every law enforcement agency is looking for you. No one can help you because they'd be aiding and abetting a known terrorist."

Marco had not thought of the repercussions. "I'm not a terrorist."

"Yes, you are. You are alone now, Marco. You have nowhere to turn. For such a book-smart kid, you're really stupid. You have to turn yourself in to the authorities."

Marco refused, "I'm not doing that."

Emphasizing the gravity of the situation, Carlo said, "Then, they will hunt you down and kill you. Do you understand what I'm saying to you? They will kill you."

Flippant, Marco said, "What does it matter then? I have nothing left to lose."

CHAPTER 29

S ARA and Phil entered their hotel room. The maid had rearranged and consolidated the vases of wildflowers while they were out.

Inhaling the scent of the blooms, Sara commented, "This is exactly what I need after the insanity of today."

Slipping his arms around her waist, Phil said, "After the day we've had, I think spending a nice quiet evening together is the way to go."

Sara noticed a bottle of Prosecco chilling by the bedside. "I could use a glass of that right about now."

He joked, "Or two, or three."

Sara laughed and kissed him. "Three glasses? I don't think so. Are you trying to get me drunk?"

He winked at her. "No. I can already have my way with you without getting you drunk."

Sara concurred, "That is true."

"One glass for the lady. Coming right up!"

Phil poured a glass of bubbly for her, then another for himself. "A toast, to you, my love."

Raising her glass, Sara corrected him, "A toast to us."

Phil smiled. "Okay, to us! May we live long and prosper!"

Sara laughed so hard, she nearly spat out her drink.

Feigning shock, Phil remarked, "What? Can't I quote Spock?"

"You're hysterical."

"I do my best to entertain. And I want you to relax and smile."

Sara smiled a phony smile. "How's this?"

He set his glass down and approached. "I want a real smile."

She stuck out her tongue then took another sip. She looked at him over the rim of her glass. Her eyes beckoned to him.

Phil responded by pulling her to him. With the sweet taste of sparkling wine on his lips, he kissed her deeply.

So caught up in the sensuality of the kiss, Sara dropped her half-full glass on a bouquet of flowers.

The heat between them rose steadily. Phil slipped his fingers under the straps of her maxi dress. Smoothly, he slid them off of her shoulders. Her breasts were revealed as the dress fell to her waist. She shimmied the dress and her thong off her hips and allowed them to waft to her feet.

Admiring her, he whispered, "You're so beautiful."

She helped him shed his clothes. Praising him, she said, "You're yummy."

They allowed their hands to caress and explore each other's bodies, lingering in all the right places.

Teased to the brink of ecstasy, Sara pushed Phil onto the bed. She mounted and straddled him. Urgently, she said, "I need you. Now."

Before he could respond, they became one body. They both moaned at the tremendous sensation.

Sara held on as Phil rocked her up and down, over and over. She fought to maintain control. Although, it was nearly impossible, for Phil was blessed with perfect dimensions, and he set an optimal rhythm.

What began as low purring escalated into fully-throated guttural moaning. With every breath, Sara pleaded for more.

Those primal vocalizations, coupled with her climaxing above him caused Phil to explode. Overcome with a myriad of emotions, he powered on until Sara succeeded in draining every drop of love and energy he possessed.

CHAPTER 30

E ARLY the next morning, Rose announced, "I have a mammogram appointment this morning. We have to leave now, or I'll be late."

Spaulding stood up and replied with a grunt.

At the hospital, Spaulding escorted her to the doctor's office in the OB/GYN wing of County General Hospital.

Rose said, "You can wait out here." Using her hands to demonstrate getting smushed, she continued, "The only thing I'll be battling in there is that damn mammography machine."

Spaulding nodded. "Good luck."

Sarcastically, Rose replied, "Thanks a lot."

What Spaulding did not realize was that there was a second entrance to the office. Rose walked nonchalantly through the office's waiting area to the other door. She opened it, looked both ways, and walked briskly to the elevators.

Rose exited the elevator on the third floor. Before she had left the house, she called the hospital and inquired what room Nico Moreno occupied. She searched the halls for the correct room.

Two uniformed policemen, Raul Gonzalez and Zach Foster, stood at the nurse's station.

Confidently, Rose strode past them.

Both men recognized her. "Mrs. Lazaro."

"Good morning, officers. Raul Gonzalez, good to see you back on the job after your accident."

Raul replied, "It's good to be back."

Rose asked, "Zach, how's your mother? I've been meaning to call her."

Zach answered, "She's doing much better. Hip surgery won't keep her down. I'll let her know you asked about her."

"Thank you. I'll stop by soon."

Rose continued walking down the hall to Nico's room. Without fanfare, she entered.

She heard Zach shout, "You can't go in there!"

The boy's mother turned, expecting to see a nurse. She recognized Rose from church. "Rose, this is a surprise."

"Lupita, nice to see you. I wish it were under different circumstances."

"Thank you."

Rose inquired, "How is your son, Nico, doing?"

"He just woke up. It's a miracle."

Nico's eyes widened, and he winced.

Rose said, "Yes, it's definitely a miracle."

Lupita explained, "The police were just here. Poor Nico doesn't remember anything."

With raised eyebrows, Rose questioned, "Is that right?"

Tears welling in her eyes, Lupita replied, "I'm just thankful he's okay."

The officers entered the room. Officer Gonzalez said, "Um, Mrs. Lazaro, you shouldn't be in here."

Rose replied, "I'll only be a minute. You're free to watch and learn. Did you already read him his rights?"

Officer Gonzalez attempted to argue, "Yes. But ..."

Rose held her hand up to quiet him. "Good. Listen closely then. And trust me, this will only take a minute. Then, I'll be out of your hair. I promise not to touch him."

Officer Foster said, "This is highly irregular. You need to leave."

Discounting his order, Rose said, "Life is anything but regular, dear. It will just take a minute."

Rose turned her attention to Nico.

Nico dropped his eyes. He wanted to run, but he was stuck in bed. And even if he could get up, Rose blocked the doorway.

Rose threatened, "Nico, are you going to tell your mother what happened? Or shall I?"

Confused, Lupita asked, "What are you talking about?"

Rose crossed her arms. "You've got about three seconds before I tell her. I think it would be better coming from you. Don't you think?"

Turning toward her son, Lupita questioned, "What is she talking about?"

Nico remained silent as he weighed his options. He debated which was worse, dealing with Rose or with the cops.

Lupita pressed, "Nico? Tell me."

Rose asked, "Are you really going to make me count to three?"

Her question was met with silence.

Not one to make idle threats, Rose started counting, "One."

The boy's mother implored, "Nico, tell me what happened."

Sternly, Rose counted, "Two."

Beads of sweat appeared on the teenager's forehead.

Rose warned, "You think things are bad now? You just wait. They're going to get worse around here if you don't start talking. I might not have my rolling pin or skillet with me, but I'm sure I'll find something to beat the truth out of you."

Perplexed, Lupita stared at her son, waiting for an explanation.

Rose leaned toward the boy. "Three."

The officers advanced farther in the room.

More afraid of Rose than of the police, sheepishly, Nico admitted, "We broke into her house."

Flabbergasted, Lupita asked, "You did what?"

He confirmed, "We broke into her house."

"For God's sake, why?"

Nico replied, "Marco asked me and Lou to help get revenge."

"Revenge? Oh, no! Tell me you didn't!"

Tapping her foot, Rose instructed, "Don't stop now. You're on a roll."

"Marco wanted to avenge Dad's death and all of our family's deaths. He said it was all their family's fault."

Dismayed, Lupita questioned, "So, you were going to kill Rose and her family? Was that your plan? To kill innocent people? People I know from church?"

The boy shrugged.

Lupita brought her hand up and covered her mouth in shock and horror. "And as if that wasn't already bad enough, *which it is,* you all could have died. I would be planning more funerals right now. It's bad enough I had to bury my husband. Now you want me to bury my sons too? What were you thinking?"

Burrowing deeper under the covers, he said, "I dunno. Marco told us we had to honor Dad. You told us that Marco was now the man of the house. We were doing what he wanted us to do."

Officers Gonzalez and Foster traded glances and shook their heads.

Rose added, "Did I mention that my six-year-old granddaughter was with me at the time they broke in?"

Appalled, the boy's mother replied, "Oh, no! I don't even know what to say. I'm so sorry, Rose. Are you okay? Is your granddaughter okay?"

"Yes, we're fine. We defended ourselves."

Lupita kept shaking her head. "Against my idiot sons! I've never been so ashamed in my life. I didn't raise them this way."

Rose patted Lupita's shoulder. "I'm sure you didn't."

Lupita turned to Nico. "You were going to kill a six-year-old child and her grandmother? What do you have to say for yourself?"

Meekly, he replied, "I'm sorry?"

Lupita reprimanded, "I'm sorry? That's it? And worse, you said it as a question instead of a statement. Dear Lord, where did I go wrong with you?"

Flippant, he said, "Okay. I'm sorry then. What else do you want me to say?"

Lupita answered, "Oh, it's more than just what you're supposed to *say*, it's what you're going to *do* that matters."

Rose said, "Officers, I assume you can take it from here?"

Officers Foster and Gonzalez replied, "Yes, ma'am."

Rose came around the corner and greeted Spaulding, "Miss me?"

Spaulding looked at Rose and then at the door he had been guarding. "Let me guess, you didn't have an appointment today."

Proud of her deception, she said, "No. But I got something better."

He exclaimed, "Geez! What did you do now?"

Waving her hand, she answered, "Oh, don't get all bent out of shape. I was just performing a public service."

He inquired, "Should I call for backup?"

"No, the police were already there. They took care of it."

Spaulding held his head. "I'm almost afraid to ask. Took care of what?"

"I got a confession out of that Nico Moreno."

At his wits' end, Spaulding asked, "You didn't beat it out of him, did you?"

"No. I used my words and not my fists. He was lucky."

Spaulding scolded Rose on the drive home. "You're not supposed to go rogue on me. I'm responsible for keeping you safe. I can't do that if I don't know where you are! Do you understand that?"

Rolling her eyes, Rose replied, "Roger. Copy. Whatever."

Protecting this woman tested Spaulding's patience and fortitude. At times, she was her own worst enemy. He silently prayed the ordeal would be over soon.

CHAPTER 31

WHILE disassembling the wounded drone, Marco Moreno's left leg bounced rapidly. That leg bounced when he was nervous, when he studied, when he took exams, and when he concentrated strongly on a task.

The impact of the bullet obliterated the camera. So, he was forced to replace it with a new one. Two of the arms of the device had also been damaged. None of the pieces were salvageable. Luckily, he had plenty of spare parts at his disposal.

As he installed the new pieces of equipment, he muttered to himself, "Okay. I'm down, but I'm not out. That was a trial run. I will succeed next time. And I'll show them all."

After his cousin's visit, his desire for revenge climbed even higher. He had to prove Carlo wrong. And he was sure that someone in the family would provide shelter for him or help him get someplace safe.

Although, carrying out his plan would be more difficult now. The Lazaro family was on high alert. Police and government agencies were involved.

Marco knew he would only have one last opportunity to strike the fatal blow. The only problem was that he had to verify the new equipment was functional. So, he would have to take it out for a quick diagnostic flight.

Marco was also aware that the authorities would be on the lookout for him. Even if he disguised himself, a lone drone pilot operating within the city limits would be a suspect. His eyes brightened as he came up with a solution.

A group of amateur drone enthusiasts congregated several times a week in a ten-acre park near the regional airfield. The airport operator and the club members signed a written agreement that they could fly their drones in the park, provided they did not cross over the fence that had been erected around the airfield. In the two years of the agreement, the fence line had never been breached.

Marco frequented this park often while developing the drone software and hardware. Since he was working on assignment, he never revealed the company he worked for or his real name.

Additionally, he made sure to launch and retrieve the drone near his car. That way, no one could see the modifications up close. And he piloted the drone at a higher altitude than the others. So, there was no way for the amateurs to know what he was doing.

He checked the calendar on his cell phone. Today was one of the days the club members met.

"What better way to slow down law enforcement than to blend in with a pack of drone geeks? Brilliant!"

CHAPTER 32

PHIL awakened before Sara. He glanced to his left. She slept on her side, facing him. The bed sheets were in a heap on the floor. He admired her nude body. He had fantasized about her and all of the things they would do when they consummated their relationship.

However, the sublime level of their intimacy surprised him. He knew it would be good. But he had no idea of how good. Even now, he struggled with the reality of it.

He had thought he and his wife had had a wonderful loving bond. Phil hated to admit it, but it paled in comparison to the intensity of what he felt with Sara.

He brushed the hair out of her face. He thought, *The face of an angel.*

Sara stirred and rolled onto her back.

He sighed. *With the body of a goddess.*

Never before had he gravitated to someone with this level of intense passion and desire. He loved her, but he lusted after her as well. He did not want to dominate her. He longed to ravish her. He loved the way she approached physicality and sensuality with reckless abandon. He had not experienced that before, but now that he had a taste of it, he was addicted.

Fully erect and aching for her, he kissed her full lips.

Sara opened her eyes.

His sleeping beauty was awake, and she smiled at him. Curling her index finger several times, she said, "Kiss me again."

As Phil kissed Sara, instinctively, his right hand caressed her left breast. He rubbed his thumb against her nipple. It perked up.

His hand wandered to the other breast and tended to it until it livened up as well. He glided over her stomach and abdomen. *God, her skin is so smooth.*

Sara sighed happily.

Swept up in the moment, he closed his eyes and allowed his hand to part her legs. He massaged her gently.

Sara moaned. "Mmm ..."

He smiled.

She thought, *What a way to wake up.*

Phil's fingers pleasured her.

She felt every inch of him against her leg. She reached over and began stroking him.

He groaned.

Sara sat up, flipped over, and got on her hands and knees. She glanced over her shoulder at him with a come-and-get-me look.

Without hesitation, he got on his knees behind her. "Are you a *Kama Sutra* girl? Every time it needs to be a different position or something?"

"Huh! I hadn't thought of that. I'm all for getting a copy of the book and trying it out."

"I'm game, sweetheart. Just try not to kill me."

She giggled. "I'll try not to. But to be on the safe side, you better eat your Wheaties."

Taking command of her hips in both hands, he plunged into her again and again. He loved to watch from this angle. It was amazing to see the way she opened up herself to him.

The view was also perfect for teasing her. Pushing in slightly, he said, "I'm just giving you a little taste for now."

This deprived her of the pleasure she yearned. "I need more. You know I need to feel all of you."

"I know exactly what you need, sweetheart."

She demanded, "Then give it to me."

"You're always in a rush."

Frustrated, Sara backed into him. Not expecting it, he penetrated her completely. Once there, he enjoyed the sensations too much to stop.

Sara smiled. She got exactly what she wanted.

Phil rocked Sara's world. His urgent rhythm betrayed his true desire.

Sara straightened up and leaned back to kiss him.

Phil admired her flexibility. He needed release, but he knew she was not ready yet. His hands dove down.

Sara felt his strong fingers pleasure a crucial spot. *Oh, dear God, that's good. So good.*

She urged, "Right there. Oh, you've got it."

Phil felt her body relax as she surrendered to him. He would not disappoint her.

Sara began to writhe as the pleasure built within her. She demanded, "Don't stop!"

Phil obeyed with renewed vigor.

She moaned much louder and dropped down on her elbows as she climaxed. She clutched the bed sheets tightly.

Phil felt the increased wetness as her body spasmed. He fought to hold on as long as possible. He wanted to make sure she was satisfied before he allowed himself to succumb.

However, the way Sara milked him was beyond compare. When she contracted her pelvis muscles to tighten her hold on him, he lost concentration. Before he realized it, he erupted with the force of a volcano.

Phil grunted and groaned exuberantly.

Sara loved Phil's noisy, primal side. "Give me every drop. I want it all."

Her greedy wish was his command. And after a few minutes, they collapsed in hot, steamy ecstasy.

She panted. "Good morning."

Breathing hard, he chuckled. "Good morning."

Sara asked, "Is that how we're going to start every day?"

Spooning her, he replied, "That's my plan. Unless you have a better one."

She giggled. "I think whoever wakes up first should be responsible for setting the plan."

He agreed, "I can live with that. So, if you wake up first, what's your plan?"

She teased, "For me to know, and you to find out."

Embracing her, he replied, "I'm looking forward to that."

CHAPTER 33

TONY handed the keys to his safe house and a set of car keys to his brother, Joe. "Okay, here are all the keys you'll need. We've gone over the route to reach the safe house. Any questions on the route?"

Joe accepted the keys. "No, I've got it."

Looking around, Sully asked, "Where's your daughter?"

Joe answered, "She's upstairs in her room, playing."

Sully said, "Good. The mall opens shortly. Spaulding will drive you all to the mall. He'll oversee the transfer."

Rose said, "Helen is going to meet us there. That way she and her car won't be on that maniac's radar at all. She can take Flora to New York City and visit with family until the entire ordeal is over."

Sully said, "We're counting on Marco to track your cell phones to monitor your whereabouts. So, we're going to have you hand off your phones to plainclothes officers when you get into the parking garage. They'll walk around the mall, making it look like you're shopping."

Tony added, "If he thinks you're shopping, he won't be looking for you anywhere else. It will give you enough time to get to the safe house."

Sal complimented, "Smart. Good idea."

Sully's phone vibrated. He glanced at the screen. "Ashby has confirmed the cars are in position in the underground garage. Helen Scotto just arrived. The plainclothes officers have been briefed. It's go time."

Tony hugged and kissed his mother. "Don't worry. Everything will be fine. Love you."

Rose said, "I'd feel better if you were coming with us."

"Marco's not going to believe we're all going to the mall together. Besides, I rarely go to the mall."

Concerned, she asked, "Where are you going?"

Tony said, "I'm staying with the team."

Sully explained, "We need your son with us. We're one man down as it is, because Ashby's going with you. He needs time to recover from his injuries anyway. He can't work as effectively in the field while he's wounded."

Irritated, Rose asked, "So, you're sending a lame duck to protect us? Wonderful! I'm going to get my handgun."

Sully replied, "There's no need for that. Ashby is not a lame duck. I have complete confidence that he can protect you."

Tony added, "The safe house is fully stocked with weapons. Ashby can show you how to use what's there, if a situation presents itself. But, hopefully, it won't come down to that."

Sal commented, "Sounds like all the bases are covered then."

Sully said, "We need to get moving. Get Flora ready to go. Grab your bags, load up, and move out."

Tony and Joe loaded all of the bags in the SUV.

Sal helped Rose and Flora into the backseat of the SUV. Joe sat up front.

Checking his watch, Sully said, "Time's wasting. Spaulding, once you complete the transfer, we'll regroup here."

Spaulding said, "Roger. Everybody buckle up. We're headed out."

Once they left, Sully said, "Lupita Moreno has agreed to help us capture her sons, Marco and Lou."

White asked, "How?"

Sully replied, "She tracked down Lou at a friend's house. The police have two units en route. So, for all intents and purposes, he's taken care of. The bigger challenge is Marco."

White inquired, "What's the plan to nab him?"

Sully responded, "She says that the Charger he's driving is in her name. It was cheaper for insurance. So, that's a dead end. And she doesn't have an address for him. She says he's shacked up with his nymphomaniac girlfriend in an apartment in the city."

Amused, Lee asked, "Does the nympho have a name? I can look her up."

Sully answered, "Only a first name, Jenny."

As hard as Tony tried, the phone number, 867-5309, and the catchy Tommy Tutone song from the 1980s, played in his head.

Sully continued, "She's going to call Marco to update him on Nico's legal predicament. The story is that Nico's not talking, and he hasn't implicated Lou or Marco."

Curious, White asked, "How about the police and the media?"

Sully answered, "The police aren't releasing any information. So, we don't have to worry about any outside interference."

Pointing out the obvious, Lee said, "Marco isn't stupid. We're not going to be able to track his phone."

Sully replied, "We know that. We're not going to even try. She's going to try to get him to come home."

Doubtful, Lee said, "I don't think he'll fall for that either."

Sully responded, "Well, there's no harm in trying. TJ's cousin, Vinnie Varone, will coach Lupita through it. In the meantime, we need to get ready."

CHAPTER 34

VINNIE sat with Lupita in her kitchen. She was visibly nervous.

Vinnie coached her, "Remember what we talked about. Try to get him to meet you."

Lupita nodded as she dialed her son's number. It rang three times.

Picking up, Marco answered, "Hi, Mama."

"Hello, Marco."

Marco asked, "How's Nico?"

"Your brother is now in jail. I'm so worried. He's underage, but they're talking about moving him to the adult jail. He won't survive with those criminals. He's a baby. I can't believe this is happening."

"You got him a good lawyer, right?

"I think so."

"I'm sure he's going to be fine."

She asked, "When are you coming home?"

"I can't. I'm busy."

"But you promised."

"I can't."

Attempting guilt, Lupita said, "Please? I'm really worried. I can't find Lou. I need you to help me find your brother."

Marco lied, "I'm really tied up with work. He'll turn up. He's probably at a friend's house."

Piling on more guilt, she said, "Maybe. But what if something has happened to him too? I don't know what I'd do. And I just can't stand to be all alone in the house. You know how I get when I'm alone. Please, come home."

"I know, but I can't."

Thinking quickly, she said, "I can come to you. I can bring you dinner. I'll make your favorite, my homemade macaroni and cheese."

He paused. He loved his mother's macaroni and cheese. "Not tonight. Maybe tomorrow."

"I wouldn't take up much time. I miss you. And is it that outlandish that I want to see my son? I haven't seen you in weeks. I need your help with this mess. You're the man of the house. You're supposed to be here when I need you. And right now, I need you. You're becoming a stranger. You're never here anymore. I don't even know what's going on in your life and what you're doing now."

Marco did not want to believe his mother was working with the authorities. However, he knew they would pressure her to cooperate. Her pleas to have him come home and see her were probably scripted. And she was pulling out all of the stops. As a result, he said, "Really, I can't right now. Another time, Mama. I need to get back to work."

Sadly, Lupita replied, "Okay. Just remember that I love you. No matter what. I love you."

Marco recognized that as the truth. His mother did love him. "I love you, too, Mama. See you soon."

The call disconnected.

Vinnie said, "You did good, Lupita. Really good."

Discouraged, she replied, "But I failed. That might have been the last conversation I'll ever have with him. And I might never see him alive again."

Vinnie said, "I know it's hard. Try to be positive. We knew it was a long shot. It's not your fault. You did the best you could. There's still a chance this could end peacefully. It's all up to him. You did your best. That's all we could ask."

With a heavy heart, she nodded.

On the other side of town, Lou Moreno was apprehended at his best friend's house. He gave up his brother, Marco, as soon as they secured the handcuffs around his wrists and Mirandized him. He even provided the name of the apartment complex of where Marco and Jenny lived. He did not know the apartment number, but he was able to pinpoint where Marco had parked his damaged Charger.

CHAPTER 35

L EE searched the apartment building's online website for registered tenants. There were only two Jennifers listed. One was seventy-eight years old. The other was twenty-two years old.

Lee pulled up the twenty-two-year-old's New York State driver's license. With two more clicks, he had Jennifer Amos' license plate number, car registration, and insurance information.

He said, "We have everything we need to find Jennifer Amos, and subsequently, Marco Moreno."

Tony said, "He'd be an idiot to drive his flashy Charger, especially since he's missing a back window. He can't rent a vehicle because he's wanted. A driving service or taxi wouldn't work either. Even if he paid cash, there would be a record of him getting picked up and dropped off. So, the only option left is his girlfriend's car. So, let's put an APB out on her car."

Lee nodded. "On it."

CHAPTER 36

ACCORDING to his cousin, Carlo Fuentes, Marco was a wanted terrorist. Based on the phone call with his mother, Marco knew something there was off. Marco was convinced that she was being watched and coached. She was of no value to him. His brand-new car was also of no value to him now.

Marco's only choice for transportation was Jenny's car. Luckily, she was still sound asleep. He did not have to come up with another story.

He rummaged in her purse for her keys. Not only did he find keys, he found a loaded handgun. He slipped that into his waistband, just in case.

Marco deposited the repaired drone and the second bomb in the trunk of the Mazda Miata. It was not as large as the original bomb. He did not have time to buy additional supplies. But it would still accomplish his objective.

He swatted the sparkling pink strands of beads that hung from the rearview mirror. They were too tangled to remove. Otherwise, he would have removed them immediately.

He pried off the fuzzy pink steering wheel cover and tossed it in the backseat. He planned to strip off the seat covers when he had more time.

Then Marco remembered a saying that his mother loved to quote. "Beggars can't be choosers."

Indeed, Marco was a beggar at the moment. Grimacing, he backed the car out of the parking spot.

CHAPTER 37

SPAULDING drove Sal, Rose, Joe, and Flora to the shopping mall in a black Chevy Suburban. He pulled into the underground parking structure as planned.

Ashby, Helen, and four plainclothes officers waited by the transfer vehicles.

Spaulding ordered, "Okay, everybody out."

Flora was the first one out. She ran to greet her other grandmother, Helen. "Hi, Nana!"

Helen embraced her. "Are you ready to go to New York City?"

Flora replied, "Yes, I'm all packed and everything."

Joe handed Flora's suitcase to Helen. He knelt down to hug Flora. "Be a good girl for your grandmother."

Confidently, Flora said, "I will."

"That's a good girl. Have fun."

Rose said to Helen, "Keep her safe."

Helen promised, "I will."

Joe informed her, "We won't have phone service any time soon. But we'll call as soon as we can. Okay?"

Helen answered, "Okay. I'm praying for all of you."

Rose replied, "Thank you. God knows we need all of the prayers we can get."

Joe hugged Flora tightly. "I love you, Flora."

"I love you, Daddy."

Flora squeezed Rose. "Love you, Grandma. Bye!"

Choking back tears, Rose responded, "Love you, too, Flora!"

Helen suggested, "We better get going."

Rose said, "Have a safe trip."

With heavy hearts, they watched Helen and Flora drive away.

Breaking the silence, Rose said, "She'll be safe with Helen. We should go."

Spaulding asked, "Do you need help with the bags?"

Joe replied, "No. We've got them."

Sal and Joe dragged eight bags out of the back of the SUV.

Dismayed, Spaulding said, "You were supposed to pack light."

Rose said, "This *is* light. I only have one tray of lasagna, one pan of ziti, some brownies, the leftover cookies …"

Spaulding had heard enough. He held up his right hand. "Okay. I get it. Forget that I said anything."

The older car had plenty of trunk space. Joe and Sal had room to spare.

Spaulding said, "I need your phones."

Joe and Rose produced their phones and turned them over to Spaulding.

Sal asked, "Rose, do you have my phone in your purse?"

Rose performed a quick search and produced the old flip phone.

Handing it to Spaulding, Sal said, "I hate cell phones. I don't even know if it still works. It's not charged. I never use it."

Joe said, "I haven't seen one of those in years. You need a new phone."

Sal replied, "It's up to your mother. She's the one who ends up carrying it."

Shaking his head, Spaulding joined the plainclothes officers and gave them the phones. After a brief exchange of words, the officers walked toward the mall entrance.

Moving more slowly than normal, Ashby addressed the Lazaro family. "I'll be following a block behind you, just to make sure we're not being physically followed. And Lee will be monitoring our route to identify any threats, aerial or otherwise."

Assessing Ashby, Rose asked, "Are you feeling up to the job?"

Ashby declared, "Yes, ma'am. I'm sworn to protect you. And I will."

Still skeptical, she said, "Good to hear."

Ashby informed them, "You've got one disposable cell phone in the glove box for an absolute emergency. And before you ask what an absolute emergency is, it means you're under fire or someone is dying. Understood?"

They replied, "Yes."

Ashby continued, "If either of those situations occur, there are two numbers programmed in, mine and Lee's. You can't call anyone else. Any questions before we go?"

Joe asked, "Will we have to stop for gas?"

"No. The tanks are full. We're driving straight there. No stops."

Rose commented, "Good thing I went to the bathroom before we left."

Ashby asked, "Anything else?"

Rose asked, "Are there basic necessities, like milk and butter, at this safe house?"

Ashby answered, "Tony said he took care of everything like that. We should be fine for a week or so."

Rose responded, "I hope to God I'm not stuck in the woods in a cabin with all of you for a week."

Spaulding was pleased to not be accompanying them on this adventure. To Ashby, he said, "Good luck, and Godspeed, my friend."

Ashby replied, "Thanks."

Spaulding chuckled as he walked away.

Ashby reiterated, "Remember, go straight to the cabin. No stops."

Joe confirmed, "Got it."

Ashby said, "Okay. I'll be right behind you the whole way. See you there."

CHAPTER 38

AFTER an evening and morning of lovemaking, Phil and Sara showered and readied themselves for their flight home.

Sara finished packing her suitcase.

Phil called out from the bathroom. "Is my ditty bag out there? I can't seem to find it."

"Let me look." Sara walked around to Phil's side of the bed. It was on the lower shelf of the nightstand. It was partially zipped. She shouted, "Found it! It was on the nightstand."

At that moment, Phil remembered something. He rushed out of the bathroom.

Sara held the bag out to him.

When he grabbed it, the bag tipped over. The contents fell on the floor.

"Oops!" Sara bent down to help Phil collect the items.

Phil attempted to dissuade her. "It's okay. I'll take care of it."

Collecting the items closest to her, she apologized, "Sorry. I should have supported the bag from the bottom."

He persisted, "Really, I've got it. You can go back to packing your stuff."

Amidst the deodorant, toothbrush, toothpaste, brush, cologne, and nail clippers, there was a small crimson box.

Sara picked up the box. She questioned, "What's this?"

Grabbing for it, he lied, "It's nothing."

She held it up high, behind her. "Are you sure it's nothing?"

Phil sighed.

Sara saw the disappointment in his eyes. She lowered the box and handed it to him. "Sorry."

Sitting on the edge of the bed, he replied, "There's nothing for you to be sorry about."

She sat on the bed next to him and kissed him on the cheek.

Pondering his options, he chuckled. "Okay. This was supposed to go differently. But what the hell?"

"Huh?"

Phil opened the crimson box and shook out a smaller, velvet-covered box, of the same color, into his hand. He got down on one knee and opened it. "Sara, will you marry me?"

The most beautiful diamond ring she had ever seen sparkled up at her. Initially, she was stunned. After a second, she starting jumping up and down. "Yes! Oh, Phil! Yes!"

Phil was thrilled with her response.

She continued, "Oh, my God! I can't believe it!"

Tickled with her reaction, he asked, "Do you think you can stop jumping long enough for me to put it on your finger?"

Ecstatic, she replied, "Of course!"

She held out her hand, and he gracefully slid the ring on her finger. Before looking at it again, she threw her arms around him and kissed him passionately.

Her excitement was overwhelming. She felt as if she could literally bounce off the walls. "I love you! I love you! I love you!"

Laughing at her exuberance, he said, "I love you, too, Sara."

Admiring the ring, she said, "It's gorgeous! Oh, look how it shimmers! No matter how the light hits it, it's spectacular!"

He acknowledged, "That's one of the reasons why I bought it."

Feeling mildly guilty, she said, "Sorry I ruined whatever you had planned."

Wrapping his arms around her waist, he said, "Sweetheart, I've been carrying this around for weeks waiting for the right moment."

She draped her arms over his shoulders. "Did you say you've had it for weeks?"

Kissing her neck, he said, "I had planned to do something in

Hawaii next week, but we're not going back there. So, I didn't really have anything else planned. And honestly, the only important part is you giving me your answer."

Amazed, she asked, "You bought the ring before we had sex?"

He revealed, "I didn't need to have sex with you to know I love you and want to spend the rest of my life with you."

"Seriously?"

He resumed kissing her neck. "Yes, seriously."

Astonished, she remarked, "Wow! I don't know what to say."

He joked, "And I figured if you were lousy in bed, I'd have plenty of time to retrain you."

Sara grabbed the nearest pillow and hit him several times. "Retrain me? Are you kidding?"

Shielding his head with his upraised arm, he shouted, "Uncle! Uncle!"

She smacked him a few more times.

Laughing, he tackled her. She fell on the bed. He held her down. "For the record, you don't need any training in that department. But after we get that sex book, I might change my mind."

Not able to move, she stuck out her tongue.

He warned, "Honey, you better not stick out that tongue, unless you're willing to use it."

She stuck out her tongue again.

He leaned over and kissed her deeply.

They were both riled up when he abruptly stopped and walked away.

Confused, she asked, "Is there a problem?"

Mischievously, he replied, "No. I just needed to warm you up."

She protested, "Oh, I'm definitely warmed up. Get back here!"

He refused, "I wouldn't want to wear you out."

She testified, "I've got all sorts of energy."

"That's what I'm counting on. We're joining that club you've always wanted to join on my jet later."

Intrigued, she uttered, "Ooo ..."

He winked at her. "Thought you might like that."
"I can't wait!"

CHAPTER 39

S PAULDING returned to the Lazaro home. With a slight spring in his step, he said, "Transfer went off without a hitch. They're on their way to the safe house. Plainclothes are mulling around the mall."

Lee added, "So far, they're not being followed."

Sully replied, "Good."

Happily, Spaulding offered, "I'm getting coffee. Anyone need anything from the kitchen?"

Everyone turned and stared at him.

Spaulding asked, "What?"

Tony remarked, "You don't seem like your usual self."

Spaulding apologized, "Forgive me for saying this, but I feel as if a weight has been lifted off my shoulders. Your mother was killing me."

Tony stated, "Imagine living with that every single day of your life."

Matter-of-factly, Spaulding said, "I would have run away."

The team members laughed.

Tony said, "She would have hunted you down."

Sully interjected, "Okay, enough of that. We need to get down to business. Lee, you'll be with me. We'll pick up the drone company's technician on the way to Jennifer Amos' apartment. You'll be responsible for bringing the tech up to speed."

Lee responded, "No problem. Got it."

"Spaulding, White, and TJ, you're in the other vehicle. Lee will give you the address. It's go time. Roll out."

The task force mobilized and picked up the drone technician, Ravi Gupta.

Lee brought Gupta up to speed on the operation.

Gupta informed them, "I launched one of our other drones, so we have an extra set of eyes. But I have to be careful not to fly too low. These units are vastly different from the average drone. Marco will spot it instantly. If worse comes to worse, my drone has been equipped with a self-destruct option. I have been authorized to destroy both units if necessary."

Sully said, "Good to know we have that option."

Lee remarked, "That's pretty drastic though."

Gupta explained, "The owners do not want anyone using their product to drop bombs on innocent people. It's bad press. So, they've authorized me to do whatever is necessary to end the threat. Obviously, they'd like their prototypes back safe and sound. But if that can't happen, I must be prepared."

Sully said, "Okay, then. Everyone is on the same page."

Gupta added, "But since I'm hoping we can go the passivist route, I've been writing code to hack the drone and assume control over it. I'm almost finished."

"Good. We're on our way to his apartment now."

Optimistically, Gupta said, "Well, if that's the case, then I can take physical possession of the equipment and bring it back to the lab."

Lee laughed. "You're assuming that he's there, *and* that he'll be willing to cooperate. In my experience, that never happens."

"Never happens? So, what normally happens?"

Handing Gupta a bulletproof vest, he replied, "Here, put this on."

Wide-eyed, Gupta asked, "We're going to get shot at?"

"It's a definite possibility."

Spaulding's SUV entered the parking garage. Sully parked in the street, across from the structure.

After a few minutes, Spaulding reported, "We've located the

Charger. No sign of the girlfriend's Miata. We're going to proceed to the apartment now."

Sully confirmed, "Roger."

Tony pounded on the apartment door. "FBI! Open up!"

A door down the hall opened. An older woman peered out.

Spaulding yelled, "Get back inside!"

The woman gave him a sour expression before she disappeared into her unit.

Spaulding kicked in the door.

White, Tony, and Spaulding entered the apartment. They cleared the main living space and kitchen. Both bedroom doors were closed.

Spaulding said, "I'll take this one. You two take the other one."

Tony tested the door knob. It turned. He pushed it open.

Jenny was spread eagle on the bed, pleasuring herself with one of her sex toys.

Before she registered what was happening, White asked, "Jenny Amos?"

Jenny responded, "Maybe. Who the hell are you?"

Tony replied, "FBI."

Jenny challenged, "You got ID?"

White and Tony flashed their badges.

Nodding, Jenny asked, "Okay, FBI. I'm Jenny. What do you want?"

White asked, "Could you please turn that off, and put some clothes on?"

They heard Spaulding kick in the other door. He yelled, "Clear!"

Jenny complained, "I'm in the middle of something. Can't you wait until I'm done?"

Outraged, White yelled, "No! Stop right now!"

Jenny switched off the toy and sat up. "You people are killjoys."

Tony averted his gaze.

White said, "We're looking for Marco Moreno. Where is he?"

Jenny stood and strutted by them naked. "I don't know."

They followed her into the main living area.

Trying hard not to stare at her accentuated curves, Tony asked, "Did you give him your car?"

Searching her purse, she replied, "I didn't give him anything. But my car keys are gone and so is my gun."

White inquired, "You have a permit for that gun?"

Jenny shimmied so her breasts swung back and forth. "Of course. I have to protect my assets, if you know what I mean."

Looking away, Tony asked, "Do you know what time he left?"

Truthfully, Jenny responded, "No. I was sleeping. We had a long night. I was tired."

Spaulding interrupted, "That other room is filled with materials to make homemade bombs."

Jenny protested, "There's no way."

Spaulding sized up the pink-haired naked woman. "Sorry, but you're wrong."

"I can't believe it."

Walking past them all, Spaulding entered Jenny's bedroom. After a moment, he located a robe. Rejoining them, he threw the robe at Jenny. "Put this on. Now!"

Jenny liked Spaulding. She admired his bulging muscles and his take-charge attitude. "Yes, sir!"

White asked, "So, you're telling us that you had no idea that Marco was making bombs in your apartment?"

Enrobed, Jenny sat on the couch. "That's what I'm telling you. He's into kinky stuff, and he's insatiable sexually. But other than that, I know he works a lot. If we're not having sex, he's locked in that room by himself. He even changed the lock on the door. I don't have a key to the new lock. He wouldn't give me one."

Frustrated, White asked, "You didn't find it odd that he refused to give you a key?"

Smirking, Jenny remarked, "In my world, people have locks and keys for all sorts of things. Some like to share, others don't. It's not unusual."

"But he's living in your apartment."

"For now. He just wants to get his rocks off. And I'm offering him a creative place to do that. We get high on weekends. We fuck a lot. That's it. There's no exclusivity. No relationship. We're experimenting. So far, he likes what I've exposed him to. Eventually, he'll move on. I don't care either way."

White commented, "That's sad."

Jenny replied, "It is what it is."

"You're too young to be this jaded."

"I've been on my own since I was fourteen. My parents caught me having a sex toy orgy with a few friends. They decided I was a freak and needed therapy. I ran away. It didn't take long to find others like me. It's a very welcoming community. We don't judge. We just like having fun. And when I met Marco, he asked me to teach him how to have fun. We're both getting something out of it. So, why not?"

White sighed.

"And just to be clear, I'm not into killing and making bombs. That's not what my circle of friends and I are about. Whatever crazy bomb stuff Marco was into, that had nothing to do with the rest of us. I swear."

White believed her.

Spaulding reported to Sully and Lee, "We're going to need a team to process the apartment. We found bomb materials in a bedroom."

Lee answered, "Dispatching now."

CHAPTER 40

AS soon as Spaulding's team reported that Marco had left the building, Lee pulled up the traffic cameras in the area. He spotted Jenny's red Miata leaving the parking structure an hour prior to their arrival. He tracked the car's movements.

Lee said, "I've tracked him to within two miles of a regional airport. There are two roads to choose from, neither have any cameras."

Gupta said, "He went to the park, next to the airfield."

Sully inquired, "How do you know that?"

Gupta typed as he answered, "Because we go there all the time."

All of the team members wore body armor under their clothes and were combat-ready. When they pulled into the gravel parking lot, they were surprised at the number of vehicles and people in the area.

Lee handed Gupta an in-ear receiver. "We're all connected through these. So, you'll need to wear it."

Gupta accepted it and inserted it in his ear. "Cool. Got it."

Sully ordered, "Lee and Gupta, you stay put. Everyone else, roll out."

They exited the two vehicles.

White exclaimed, "Wow! This is quite a crowd."

Spaulding commented, "We didn't expect a convention. There must be close to one hundred people out here."

White added, "Predominantly male. Most wearing T-shirts and baseball hats."

Tony commented, "Wonderful."

White asked, "Isn't it a bad idea to have all these drones so close to an airfield?"

Gupta replied, "The operator of the airfield has a written agreement with the drone pilots. As long as they stay on this side of the fence and don't fly above a certain altitude, they're fine. Actually, we use this area all the time to test our drones."

Spaulding said, "That's stupid." He paused. "What's our next move?"

Sully directed, "Locate Moreno, and proceed as planned."

Tony pointed out, "That's going to be more challenging with this crowd. We don't have drones, so we can't just blend in."

Spaulding asked, "Are you saying you're not up for the task?"

Tony replied, "No. It's just going to be challenging, and I want to limit the collateral damage. That's all. And we have no idea what this guy might do if he's cornered."

Sully asked, "Anybody have eyes on Moreno?"

A chorus of, "Negative," followed.

Sully questioned, "Lee, not even with your facial recognition software?"

Frustrated, Lee said, "A lot of the guys are wearing ballcaps. We'd have to fly the drone a lot lower to get a better angle. And we can't do that, like Gupta said, because Marco will recognize one of the company's drones immediately."

Spaulding opened the driver's door on the SUV, reached in, and popped the hood. He pretended to investigate an engine problem.

Strolling leisurely through the lot, Tony said, "I found the Miata. Doors locked. Ugly pink fuzzy interior. Nothing of value in plain sight."

After a few minutes, Spaulding reported, "Got him. North side of the field. Gray T-shirt, blue jeans, faded blue baseball cap."

Tony concurred, "I see him."

Sully ordered, "Move in. Surround him."

Spaulding dropped the hood closed.

In unison, they replied, "Roger."

As instructed, Lee and Gupta stayed with the vehicles.

They observed Marco staring at the drone's controller. He made subtle movements as he ran the equipment through a series of tests.

Gupta typed furiously in an attempt to hack the drone.

The rest of the team quietly surrounded the target. It was easier than anticipated because Marco was focused on the screen in front of him.

Spaulding reported, "I have a clear shot."

Sully ordered, "Hold."

Spaulding replied, "Roger."

Sully asked, "What's the progress on controlling the drone?"

Gupta said, "I'm typing as fast as I can. I'm using a back door. But he might discover me before I finish."

Sully directed, "Make sure that doesn't happen."

Keys clacking, Gupta replied, "I'm doing the best I can."

Mingling and blending in with the crowd, White casually looked around.

Spaulding said, "Let me just take the shot and end this."

Sully replied, "Give the kid another minute."

Gupta yelled, "And ... yes!"

Lee confirmed, "We have control over the drone."

The drone abruptly changed course.

For a split second, Marco believed the drone malfunctioned. When he realized he no longer controlled the drone, he swore, threw the controller to the ground, and ran into the middle of the crowd.

Running, Spaulding said, "Lost the shot. In pursuit."

Sully ordered the team, "Go! Go! Go!"

Marco weaved in and out of the drone enthusiasts.

Sully shouted, "Stop! FBI!"

Most of the pilots stopped and looked around. Several hit the ground and covered their heads with their hands. A few ran for their cars.

Gupta flew the drone over to the SUV. Quickly, he stepped out, retrieved it, and returned to the safety of the vehicle. He declared, "Success!"

Lee said, "Good job. But it's not over yet."

Frustrated, Tony pushed his way through the crowd. "He's headed for the parking lot."

Marco sprinted through the parking lot, weaving in and out of the rows of cars to reach Jenny's Miata. He saw armed men advancing to his position. The Miata lacked the power of his beloved Charger. But the tires kicked up gravel and dust. A slow-moving car blocked the aisle. He pounded the steering wheel with his fists. "Move!"

The tactical team piled back into the SUVs and blocked the entrance to the parking lot.

Marco maneuvered around the nuisance car. He assessed his situation. Barricades flanked two sides of the lot. Armed men were blocking the only road out. There was only one option left. He floored it and veered sharply into the crowd.

Confused, the other drone pilots yelled, swore, and scrambled out of the way.

Marco headed directly for the chain link fence.

The weak links gave way but Marco ended up dragging part of the fence with him. He was now on the airport property, driving like a bat out of hell. Marco barreled through the low-lying brush and emerged in the hangar area.

One hangar door was open. A plane was situated in front of it. He accelerated toward the far side of the hangar.

CHAPTER 41

JOE and his parents entered Tony's safe house. It was dark and dreary.

Rose pulled the dusty curtains back. She opened the windows to get rid of the stale, musty odor.

Joe commented, "It's pretty basic, but Tony says it has everything we need."

Evaluating her surroundings, Rose said, "That's highly debatable. This place needs work. And lots of it."

Attempting to put things into perspective, Sal said, "It's a hideaway. It's not the Ritz, Rose."

Disgusted with the dust and grime, she asked, "Don't you think I know that?"

Sal suggested, "We need to make the best of it. Remember, it's temporary."

"Temporary or not, it's filthy. I have to clean."

Sitting on the couch, Sal said, "Knock yourself out, dear."

Joe went on a self-guided tour.

Ashby checked on the security system.

Joe whined, "There's no television."

Automatically, Rose said, "Big deal. Go play outside."

Not completely surprised by her response, Joe walked away.

Sal picked up an outdated magazine from the end table.

Rummaging under the kitchen sink, Rose found some cleaning supplies. She announced, "I'm going to start cleaning. You should all go sit on the porch. Get some fresh air."

Joe noticed the coffee table was hinged. He opened it. He

discovered it contained an old-school treasure trove of old board games, books, and decks of playing cards.

Sal glanced up from his magazine. He peered into the storage compartment. "Looks like we're going to have a lot of quality family time."

Closing the lid, Joe sighed. "I'm going outside."

Ashby warned, "Don't go far. Stay on the porch where I can see you."

Joe complained, "Geez. Even Ma let me venture a few blocks away from home."

Ashby replied, "Sorry. Times have changed. You're confined to the porch."

Joe asked, "So, I'm grounded?"

Ashby answered, "Yes. We all are. Get used to it."

CHAPTER 42

PHIL playfully pinched Sara's rear end as they climbed up the jet's stairs.

Sara threw a startled look over her shoulder.

He winked at her.

She shook her head and smiled.

He justified, "It's right in front of me. I just couldn't help myself."

Ignoring his comment, Sara settled into her leather airliner seat. "Phil, you're spoiling me completely. I never want to fly commercial ever again."

Phil laughed. "As the future Mrs. Potter, you won't have to. Make yourself comfortable while I finish loading our bags."

Alan, the pilot, checked on them. "I'm going to start my preflight checks shortly."

Phil said, "Good. It'll only take me a few minutes to load the bags."

Alan replied, "Okay. Great."

After Alan disappeared into the cockpit, Phil said, "I can't wait to start our club initiation ceremony."

Sara's eyes lit up. "Mmm hmm. Do we have to be exactly one mile up? Or can it be any altitude?"

"I'm not sure of the rules. But I'm guessing any elevation will do. You're too funny sometimes."

Sara said, "That's why you keep me around, for comedy relief!"

Phil walked toward the stairs. "Yeah, that must be it."

Stretching, Sara declared, "I just can't wait to get away from all of the drama here."

Phil joked, "Are you sure you won't miss Clear Brook?"

"After all of the crap you witnessed, you have to ask me that?"

He winked at her. "Just checking you're not a closeted drama queen."

"No. I'm not a drama queen. And I'm not going to miss Clear Brook. Not one little bit. I just want to live in the peace and tranquility you keep promising me."

Phil descended the stairs as Sara rummaged around in her purse for some chewing gum.

As Phil grabbed the last bag, he felt a gun in the small of his back. He exclaimed, "What the hell?"

Marco ordered, "Just do what I tell you, and no one will get hurt."

He turned to face his assailant. He recognized him immediately as Marco Moreno.

Marco appeared nervous and agitated. He repeatedly checked over his shoulder.

Phil offered, "If you want money, I'll give you money."

Looking for his pursuers, Marco barked, "I don't need your money. I need your plane. Drop the bag."

Phil complied and released the bag.

"Shut the cargo door."

Phil secured the door.

Marco forced Phil up the stairs, into the plane. "Up! And don't try anything."

Sara was admiring her ring when Phil reentered the plane. "I can't stop staring at it. I just love ..." She stopped and gasped when she saw Phil being held at gunpoint. "Oh, my God! It's you!"

Marco directed Phil, "Sit down."

Phil sat, grudgingly.

Marco heard talking. It took him a second to realize the pilot was communicating with someone on the radio. He ordered Phil, "Yell for the pilot, and tell him to come out here."

Stalling, Phil suggested, "Why don't you let us all go? I'll give you the plane."

Annoyed, Marco said, "I can't fly it. Call him out."

Phil glanced at Sara. She had not moved an inch.

Pointing the gun at Sara, Marco threatened, "Call him, or I'll shoot her."

Feeling he had no choice, Phil shouted, "Alan!"

As they waited for a response, Marco turned to peer out the window. He knew the people chasing him would catch up soon. And they had. He saw two black SUVs on the edge of the blacktop.

Observing that Marco was distracted, Phil kicked him with both feet and knocked him off-kilter. Phil sprang up. He intended to wrestle Marco for the gun. However, he underestimated Marco, who did not let go of the firearm.

On his back, Marco pulled the trigger. He missed Phil by an inch. The bullet lodged in the fuselage above Phil's head.

Pulling himself up, Marco winced at the pain radiating across his chest. He admonished Phil, "That was a big mistake."

Holding his hands up, Phil said, "Sorry. Can't blame a guy for trying." Phil sat down.

Nerves frayed, Marco yelled, "Don't try to be a hero! Do what I tell you to do. Or I'm going to shoot both of you."

Alan, the pilot, appeared from the cockpit. "Did I just hear a gunshot?"

Marco pointed the gun at him.

Raising his hands, Alan said, "Oh, shit."

Phil pleaded, "Let them go. You can take me hostage. But let them go."

Marco argued, "Not on your life. Three hostages are better than one. And I need someone to fly this plane."

Phil volunteered, "I can fly the plane. You only need me. Let them go."

Sara protested, "No! There's no way I'm leaving you. I can't let you do this alone."

With great concern in his eyes, he argued, "You have to go. I love you more than life itself. I'll never forgive myself if something happens to you."

Sara replied, "What about you? I love you just as much. I can't leave you."

Not wanting to hear their banter any longer, Marco complained, "Oh, cut the lovey-dovey bullshit! It makes me want to throw up."

Realizing Marco was distracted, Alan grabbed for Marco's gun. However, Marco's grip was solid. Marco knew he could not out-wrestle the pilot. So, he rammed his knee into the pilot's groin.

Alan dropped to his knees, writhing in pain.

Marco said, "You're more trouble than you're worth."

Alan looked up.

Marco aimed the gun at Alan's head and pulled the trigger.

Alan's body slumped to the floor.

Sara screamed. "Oh, my God! You killed him!"

Phil jumped up and advanced toward Marco. "You son of a bitch!"

"Sit back down, or she'll be next."

Alan had fallen in front of the stairs. Blood pooled around his head.

Marco kicked the lifeless body. He thought, *If Carlo could only see me now.*

Phil was shocked in horror. He knew he had to do everything in his power to get Sara off the plane. As calmly as possible, Phil said, "Let her go. I'll fly you wherever you want to go."

Marco realized he would fare better with only one hostage. Two conniving hostages could overpower him. Pointing the gun at Sara, he ordered, "Get up."

Angst-ridden, Sara looked at Phil. "I can't. I just can't leave you."

Phil replied, "You *have* to go."

Marco squeezed the trigger and put a bullet in Sara's seat.

Sara jumped and screamed.

Testy, Marco stated, "You can, and you will. Next time, it'll be your head."

Sara approached Marco. Alan's body blocked the way to the stairs.

Marco ordered, "Take him with you."

Confused, Sara asked, "What?"

"Take the pilot with you."

"I can't carry him down."

"Who said anything about carrying him?"

Perplexed, Sara stared at Marco.

Marco directed, "Drag him to the edge, prop him up, and I'll handle it from there."

Sara hesitated.

"Do it, or I'll blow lover boy's head off."

In her mind, Sara rationalized, *If I do what he says, he won't hurt us. Please, God. Don't let him hurt us.*

She cringed as she touched Alan's body. She refused to look at him. She wanted to remember him alive and well. Her hands were soaked in warm blood and tissue. She gagged. *Oh, Alan. I'm so sorry. There's so much blood. Oh, God! I'm sorry that he did this to you. But at least it was quick, and you didn't suffer.*

She lingered to say a prayer.

Marco yanked her to her feet and pushed her aside. Then, with a strong kick, Marco sent Alan's body tumbling down the stairs.

Sara covered her mouth with her hands, so she would not scream again.

Pleased to be rid of the dead body, Marco reached into his pocket and pulled out a cell phone. He pressed several buttons, then put it back in his pocket. "It's your turn, princess. Get the fuck off of this plane! Now!"

Sara questioned, "What did you just do?"

Smirking, Marco replied, "I programmed in all the time your friends have left down there. You better hurry, or you'll still be in the blast radius when it goes off."

Completely distraught, Sara said, "I love you, Phil."

"I love you, too. Go! Everything's going to be fine." Although, at the moment, Phil was unsure how he would fulfill that promise.

Marco taunted, "Yeah, yeah, everything's going to be great. Go!"

Sara swiftly navigated the steps.

When she reached the ground, Sully and Tony were halfway to the hangar with Alan's body.

Sara ran toward them, shouting, "It's that guy we picked out in the police photos—Marco Moreno! He's on the plane!"

Tony confirmed, "We know. We tracked him here."

Sara continued, "He has Phil as a hostage. He's going to make him fly the plane."

Tony asked, "Are you hurt?"

"No. But I think there's a bomb."

Sully asked, "Where?"

"I don't know. He punched something into his cell phone. He said he programmed in all the time you have left, and if I didn't hurry, I wouldn't be able to escape the blast zone."

Tony deduced, "The car! The bomb's in the car."

Sully directed, "Fall back, now! There's a bomb in the car."

Spaulding asked, "Time to detonation?"

"Unknown. But I'm guessing not long."

White offered, "It could be a bluff to buy time."

Sully responded, "Can't take the chance. Since we don't know what we're dealing with, fall back."

Spaulding said, "I'm getting on that plane. He's running. It's a safe bet that he's not going to blow himself up."

Sully said, "Watch your back."

"Roger."

Sully hustled Sara into the SUV with Lee and Gupta. Tony and White jumped into the other SUV. They drove away from the Miata, just in case. They parked near the end of the runway.

Sully asked, "Did Marco mention where he wants to go?"

Sara replied, "No. There was just a lot of yelling and shooting. He's unhinged."

Exiting the SUV, Sully said, "Stay inside the vehicle."

Attempting to comfort Sara, Gupta said, "I'm sure everything will be fine."

She questioned, "Who are you?"

"Ravi Gupta. Tech support."

Tears welled in her eyes, but Sara was determined not to cry. She wanted to be strong for Phil. But she could not help from worrying. *How is it going to be okay? I finally found the man of my dreams. And he could die. It's my fault for insisting we come here. I never should have come back to Clear Brook. It's been nothing but trouble.*

Holding up a bottle of water, Gupta asked, "Would you like something to drink? We've got bottled water and energy drinks."

Visibly shaken, Sara accepted the water. "Thanks."

Not knowing what else to do, Gupta patted her shoulder.

Sara appreciated the gesture. Her thoughts were flying in umpteen directions. She knew she had to calm her mind. She focused on her breathing and sipped some water.

To distract herself, Sara focused on the positive. *Phil would want me to think positively. You can't have a positive life thinking negative thoughts.*

Reconsidering her visit to Clear Brook, she thought, *It wasn't all bad. Phil and I had wonderfully romantic moments. We made love in exhilarating ways. And he proposed to me here this morning. It wasn't elaborate, but it was perfect. We're going to get married. And we're going to form a foundation for the parks. We have too many plans and dreams to fulfill for everything to end before we even get started. He just has to be okay. He just has to. Please, God. Please, let him be okay.*

CHAPTER 43

A S Marco secured the plane's door, Phil looked for something to use as a weapon and came up empty.

Marco demanded, "Okay, lover boy, get up there, and fly this plane."

Stalling, Phil inquired, "Where are we going?"

"It's none of your fucking business. Just fly."

Marco checked his phone, then looked out the window. Anger and disappointment boiled up. Another failure. *A wire must have gotten loose as I hit the fence and drove through the grass. Fuck!*

However, the mere threat of an explosion mobilized his pursuers. It was a partial win.

Phil insisted, "I need to know where we're going to know if I have enough fuel. We only put in a little more than we need. Jet fuel isn't cheap you know."

"How much did you put in?"

"I'm not the one who puts the fuel in. I don't know."

Marco watched the tactical team back off and reestablish its position at the end of the runway. He replied, "Then I guess we'll just fly until we run out of fuel then. I'm done with this. Start the engines. Let's go!"

"I have to do the preflight checks. I've never flown one of these before."

"You said you could fly."

Trying to buy time, Phil explained, "I can. I've just never flown this model. Give me a few minutes to familiarize myself with the gauges."

While scanning the gauges, out of the corner of his eye, Phil saw Spaulding hugging the side of the aircraft. That gave him hope. He needed to stall a little longer. He found the switch that controlled the cargo door. He opened it, hoping Spaulding would understand what he was doing.

There was a trap door that allowed access to the cargo hold from the cabin.

Marco demanded, "Start the engines. Now!"

Phil fired them up. He also flipped a bunch of switches and tapped the fuel gauge for show.

When Sara heard the whine of the engines, she yelled, "You have to do something!"

Not exactly a people person, Lee said, "We are."

Sara argued, "Not from where I'm sitting, you aren't."

Lee said, "It's not like I can send out an EMP to disable the plane."

Gupta added, "Right. An electromagnetic pulse would knock out everything electronic in this section of the grid. Too dangerous to try."

Lee asked, "But could you imagine if we could? How awesome would that be?"

Excitedly, Gupta replied, "It would be epic!"

Sara could not believe she was stuck in an SUV with two engineering nerds while the love of her life was in peril. She really wanted to knock their heads together. Instead, she practiced her breathing exercises.

Gupta asked Lee, "How did you get a gig like this one? Drone programming is so boring compared to this type of work."

Lee replied, "Normally, I'm not in the field like this. I'm behind the scenes. Let's just say I hacked into the wrong government website, and here I am."

Fed up, Sara interrupted, "Hello? Can you guys keep focused for one minute? The man I love is on that plane. A lunatic has a gun to his head. I need you geeks to focus!"

Lee reassured her, "We're staying on top of everything. Spaulding just snuck on the plane. He's the best we have."

As Phil fired up the engines, Spaulding quietly pushed the trap door open and hoisted himself up. He could see the two men engaged in a heated conversation. He crept forward, gun drawn.

Phil had seen a warning light. The cargo door was ajar for a moment, then the light turned off. He prayed that meant that the cavalry had arrived.

Agitated, Marco asked, "What are you waiting for?"

Phil lied, "I don't have clearance to take off yet."

Marco caught him in the lie. "There's no tower here. You fly by sight." He nudged Phil with the barrel of the gun. "So, get going."

Phil slowly eased down the access road to the runway.

Marco peered out the window.

With Marco distracted, Phil looked around for anything he could use as a weapon. *If this plane takes off, I'm probably not going to make it back alive. And I can't let that happen. I have too much to live for. And I promised Sara everything would be okay. And a Potter never breaks a promise.*

Finally, Phil felt the small fire extinguisher next to his seat. At the end of the access road, he maneuvered the plane onto the runway.

Marco screamed, "Go already!"

Phil flipped some more switches to buy time. Then he unclipped the fire extinguisher. With one swift motion, he threw it at Marco. Unfortunately, Marco saw it coming, he ducked and fired once at Phil.

The bullet connected with Phil's upper left arm. Phil grunted and grabbed for his arm. Blood blossomed on his shirt sleeve. He applied pressure, but quickly realized there were two wounds. He couldn't apply pressure on the front and back of his arm.

Marco lowered the gun. "See what you made me do?"

Phil glared at him. "Are you going to help me stop the bleeding, or are you going to watch me bleed to death?"

"What the fuck?"

"I can't fly or land this thing if I pass out from blood loss or if I'm dead."

The first aid kit was next to Marco. He shoved his gun in his front pocket. Then, he popped open the kit and found a tourniquet and the elastic wrap bandage roll. He hovered over Phil. He tied the tourniquet above the bullet wounds. The blood flow slowed. Then, Marco began to wind the bandage around Phil's arm.

Phil commented, "Looks like you've done this before."

Marco replied, "We got first aid training in Boy Scouts."

Not about to waste the opportunity, Phil rammed his elbow up into Marco's jaw.

Marco pinwheeled backward. Blood dripped out of the corner of his mouth. His eyes blazed in anger. The extinguisher was against his foot. He reached down.

As Phil stood to gain the upper hand, Marco rammed the extinguisher into Phil's gut then kicked Phil with both legs.

In cramped quarters, Phil toppled back into the pilot's seat. His arm throbbed, and he was beginning to feel lightheaded. Phil planted his right shoe in Marco's chest.

Marco felt a few ribs crack. He gasped and grabbed his chest. Despite the searing pain, he pulled out his gun. "Good thing I was paying attention earlier."

Phil was not sure what he meant until he saw what Marco did next.

Marco engaged the controls, and the plane began to move and accelerate down the runway.

Phil exclaimed, "Oh, shit!"

Marco taunted, "You're not as smart as you think you are."

Phil grabbed for the firearm. As they wrestled for control of the gun, it fired.

Marco yelped. The bullet penetrated his left leg. Undeterred, he continued fighting for control of the gun. It fired again.

This time, the bullet grazed the side of Phil's head. Blood

poured out from right above his temple down the side of his face. Phil reached up with his right hand and applied pressure to his head wound. His vision blurred.

Marco raised the gun and pressed it against Phil's forehead. Matter-of-factly, he said, "This is the end of the road for you. Prepare to die."

As the plane barreled down the runway, Sara and the team saw four bright flashes in the cockpit.

Sara screamed, "No! Oh, my God! No!"

They watched the plane skid off the end of the runway and come to a stop.

Sara and the entire team waited for confirmation of who had been shot.

Sara prayed, "Please, God, don't let it be Phil."

CHAPTER 44

SPAULDING reached the cockpit. Blood covered both men. Marco was slumped over. The gun was on the floor. Spaulding barked, "I need a medic!"

Lee replied, "Roger that. An ambulance is on its way. Two minutes out."

Kicking the gun out of the way, Spaulding shouted, "Potter? Can you hear me? Potter?"

With his feet still on the brakes, Phil held his head. Blood poured through his fingers. His clothes were saturated with blood and sweat.

Spaulding repeated, "Potter? Can you hear me?"

Dazed, Phil replied, "Yeah. Losing lots of blood though."

Spaulding directed, "Hang on. Don't move."

Phil said, "I'm not going anywhere."

Spaulding located the discarded first aid kit. He grabbed the largest pads of gauze and bandages. He applied several bandage pads to Phil's head injury and wrapped the gauze around his head. He quickly assessed the arm wound. The tourniquet was doing its job. He said, "Keep pressure on your head."

Phil gave Spaulding a thumbs-up sign.

Spaulding turned his attention to Marco. He saw that his two bullets found their marks. One blew out the left side of Marco's skull. The other went through his side and into his heart.

As part of protocol, Spaulding pressed his fingers against Marco's neck. Although, he already knew Marco was dead.

Phil said, "From the looks of him, I'm assuming he's dead."

Spaulding responded, "Affirmative. He's dead. He won't be a problem anymore."

Phil attempted to stand.

"What are you doing?"

"Trying to get up and out of this plane."

Spaulding advised, "You should wait for medical. They're on their way."

"No. I want out."

Spaulding offered, "I'll carry you out."

Phil insisted, "No. I'm climbing down those stairs under my own power."

Shaking his head, Spaulding helped Phil stand. Phil was weak and unsteady on his feet.

Approaching the plane, Sully demanded, "Report!"

Spaulding replied, "Hostile's dead. Bringing Potter out now."

Spaulding supported the majority of Phil's weight as they ambled down the stairs. When they reached the ground, Phil's legs gave way. Spaulding anticipated his collapse, so he hoisted Phil up on the awaiting gurney.

Sara ran to him. The sight of Phil's face, body, and clothes covered in blood terrified her.

Recognizing the look in her eyes, Phil reassured her, "I'm okay."

Beyond worried, she said, "But you're soaked in blood."

In a weak, yet reassuring tone, Phil replied, "It looks worse than it is. I'm fine. You saw me walking. And I'm talking. Trust me, I'm fine thanks to Spaulding."

Sara turned to address Spaulding. "Thank you. Thank you for saving him and bringing him back to me."

Spaulding answered, "All in a day's work. Glad I could be of service."

Sara continued, "I don't know how I can ever repay you."

Spaulding said, "It's not necessary. Take care."

Sara responded, "You too. Thanks again."

Spaulding nodded before walking off to rejoin his team.

Holding Phil's hand, Sara confessed, "I thought I was never going to see you again."

As the medical team assessed Phil's injuries, he joked, "You couldn't get rid of me that easily."

"I don't know what I would have done if anything happened to you."

"But nothing did, so you don't have to think about it anymore. It's over."

The female EMT said, "It looks like the bullet just grazed your head. You're really lucky."

The male EMT reported, "We've got a through and through on the arm. Stitches at a minimum."

Phil asked, "Can't you just patch me up with those Steri-Strips?"

The female EMT responded, "No. You're going to the hospital."

CHAPTER 45

THE perimeter alarms at the safe house screeched so loudly that Rose heard them over the whine of the vacuum cleaner. Switching off the vacuum, she shouted, "Where are the guns? We need guns!"

Sal and Joe looked up from the Monopoly game they were playing on the front porch.

Ashby scrambled to check the monitors. He spied one lone car driving toward the house, one mile out.

Frantic, Rose asked, "What's going on? Where are those guns? We have to defend ourselves! We need guns!"

Ashby replied, "Stay calm. It's just one car. With the condition of the gravel road and the number of twists and turns, it will take approximately ten minutes for the car to reach us."

Sal and Joe abandoned their game and joined them in front of the monitors.

Sal commented, "One car can do a lot of damage, if it's rigged with explosives."

Joe asked, "Can you zoom in?"

Ashby enlarged the image of the vehicle. "One occupant."

Rose said, "Unless more are hiding in the trunk or in the backseat to throw us off-guard. Where are the guns?"

Ashby answered, "It looks like it might be TJ."

Joe asked, "Are you positive?"

Scooting out of the way, Ashby replied, "Look for yourself."

Joe examined the image. "It's too blurry to know for sure. It could be him. But it might not be. I don't know."

Ashby said, "It's a dark sedan. It could be one from our fleet."

Rose pushed her way closer to the screen. Squinting her eyes. "Are you one hundred percent positive?"

Truthfully, he said, "No."

Rose replied, "Well, I'd rather err on the side of caution. So, don't make me ask you again. Where are the guns?"

Reluctantly, Ashby led them to the weapons stash. He lifted up the floorboards to reveal the hidden weapons.

Astonished, Joe muttered, "Wow!"

Sal whistled. "Will you look at that!"

Ashby knew they had the right to defend themselves. But he also knew that Marco Moreno was more than capable of designing a car bomb. And against a car bomb, these weapons would not do them any good. Nevertheless, he passed out the bulletproof vests.

Ashby helped Rose adjust her vest as Sal and Joe struggled with theirs.

Satisfied with the vest's fit, Rose examined her weapon options. She had logged several hours at the local shooting range. She selected a Glock pistol. It was slightly different from her own semiautomatic handgun, but it was familiar enough. After loading the magazine into the gun, Rose announced, "Locked and loaded. I'm ready to go."

Sal asked, "You've been dying to say those words since you started going for target practice, haven't you?"

Shoving another two loaded magazines in her pockets, Rose replied, "You bet. I'm going to get this bastard and end this feud, once and for all."

Handing Joe a semiautomatic rifle, Ashby said, "I'm glad she's on our side."

Joe had never held a weapon. The closest he had ever gotten was pretending to be a cowboy when he was young. The rifle was heavier than he anticipated.

Ashby passed Sal the same type of rifle. Sal had hunted rabbits and squirrels with his father, so he had some experience with a firearm.

Ashby provided a quick tutorial.

Rose's eyes were glued to the monitor. "They're almost here. I'm going out there."

Sal warned, "Rose, don't!"

She opened the door and stormed out. "None of you can stop me. I've got a gun and a vest, I'll be fine."

Sal stated, "That woman is going to be the death of me yet."

All three men rushed after her.

Ashby announced, "I would prefer defending ourselves from inside the house. At least then we'd have some cover. We're out in the open here. It's not a good position to be in. We need to go back in the house."

Rose trained her gun on the approaching vehicle. "You go back in if you want to. I'm staying here and looking this degenerate in the eyes."

Sal sighed. "I guess it's settled then. We're staying out here.

Joe added, "And we're totally screwed."

Sal nodded in agreement.

The men raised their weapons. Now, all four guns were aimed directly at the incoming vehicle.

The driver saw the welcoming party and slammed on the brakes. The car slid in the gravel and ended up canted sideways. A cloud of dust formed around the vehicle.

The tension built as the dust settled.

A single gunshot broke the silence.

The men jumped.

Rose had shot out one of the vehicle's front tires.

Ashby yelled, "Shit! What'd you do that for?"

Calmly, Rose stated, "To flatten the tire. Harder to get away with a flat."

Frustrated, Ashby replied, "While that *is* sound logic, it's totally unnecessary at this juncture."

"Well, now he knows I mean business."

Sal said, "I think he probably figured that out when he saw the guns pointed at him."

Joe murmured, "We're going to die."

Ashby declared, "No one is dying on my watch. Stay sharp, people. And don't fire unless I tell you to."

Slowly, the driver's door opened.

Ashby shouted, "Let me see your hands!"

A pair of hands emerged. Then, the driver slowly stepped out of the car. He yelled, "It's me, Anthony. Don't shoot, Ma!"

Rose shouted, "Sweet Mother of Jesus! I just shot at my own son!"

Relieved, Sal and Joe lowered their weapons.

Rose ran down the porch steps to greet her son. "Anthony! Are you okay?"

"Thanks for just shooting the tire and not me, Ma. Of course, Sully won't be happy you shot out his tire."

Gesturing, she said, "Oh, my God! I never would have forgiven myself in a million years, if I shot my own son. What's going on? Why are you here? Where are the others? Tell me they're not dead."

"There was one civilian casualty. But his injuries aren't life threatening. Everyone is okay, Ma. It's finally over. We can go home."

She questioned, "It's really over, over? Or they just *think* it's over?"

Tony confirmed, "Yes, it's completely over."

Rose challenged, "How do we know for sure? What kind of proof is there? I want certifiable, undeniable proof."

Tony explained, "Marco Moreno is dead. Spaulding shot and killed him. Lou and Nico are in jail. Lou corroborated Nico's story that the vendetta was all Marco's idea from the start. Marco promised them that there would be a big cash payout. That's why they went along with it. It was about money for them, not revenge. And to cover all the bases, we also paid another visit to Carlo Fuentes. He reassured us that there wouldn't be any further problems or bloodshed."

Relieved, Joe said, "So, back to normal."

Rose stated, "I'm not sure that we can ever feel normal again."

Sal interjected, "But we're alive and well. From here, we can pick up the pieces and move forward."

CHAPTER 46

P HIL'S doctor spoke at great length to Phil and Sara about post-traumatic stress before discharging him. The physician explained that they were most likely still in shock. However, they needed to look for signs of post-traumatic stress in the upcoming days and weeks.

After being released from the hospital, Phil did not want to spend one more night in Clear Brook. It would take weeks before his jet would be back in service. Even then, he no longer had a pilot to fly it.

Phil arranged for Alan's body to be flown back to his hometown and covered all of the funeral expenses. Alan was not just an employee, he had been a friend. And Phil could not believe that he was gone. It weighed heavily on his heart.

Phil decided to drive one of the loaned cars back to his house in the mountains. However, Sara insisted on driving, due to his current physical condition.

Staring out the side window, Phil complained, "I could have driven, you know."

Sara replied, "You were shot twice. Your arm is in a sling. You're light-headed. The doctor gave you a list of activities you're not allowed to do for the next two weeks. Driving is on the list."

Phil scoffed. "He's being overly cautious. I had worse wounds from falling off my bike when I was a kid. This is nothing. If you get tired or change your mind, I'm more than happy to drive."

Rolling her eyes, Sara said, "Duly noted."

Sara remembered driving this exact route six months ago.

Phil said, "Penny for your thoughts."

Passing a slow-moving car, she answered, "Six months ago, I drove on this road to basically run away from everything. I was a complete disaster. I had quit my job and broken up with my fiancé. I had no direction. I thought I was going to lose my mind."

Touching the bandage on his head, he said, "It's interesting how life works out sometimes."

Nodding her head, she agreed, "Yup. And it's funny how I was approaching so many major life changes and didn't realize it."

Phil pointed out, "You already started making changes before the trip. You just didn't know where you were going to end up."

"That's true. You're right."

"You could have gone back to your old life. It's obvious that Joe would have taken you back in a heartbeat. You could have gotten a job similar to the one you had. You had the choice of returning to what was familiar."

Sara steered the car back into the right lane. "Uh huh."

"But you didn't. You threw caution to the wind. And now, look at you."

She declared, "I couldn't have done it without you. You saved me, literally and figuratively."

Deflecting her praise, he replied, "Any local would have stopped to help you in that storm. I just happened to come along first."

"Fine. Minimize your heroics if you want to. But I never will. Although, I never would have guessed in a million years that we'd end up together as a couple."

Curious, he asked, "Why not?"

She stated, "You aren't my type."

He asked, "You have a type?"

Checking the rearview mirror, she replied, "Well, yeah."

Struggling to find a more comfortable position, he said, "This should be good."

She clarified, "Physically, that is."

Phil found that humorous. "Oh, really? The way you looked at me as I peeled off my muddy clothes the night we met makes me think otherwise."

Sara blushed. "Oh, God. I didn't think you noticed."

Phil chuckled. "Honey, I was afraid you were going to jump me. Your mouth was hanging open, and you were drooling."

She protested, "I was not drooling!"

He rolled his eyes. "And that's your story, and you're sticking to it."

"If you weren't injured, I'd hit you."

He smirked. "I didn't mind your drooling at all. I was flattered that a young girl like you was interested in an older guy like me."

"There's not that big of an age difference."

"There's enough."

She presumed, "And I guess that means you saw me staring at you taking a shower too."

Startled, he said, "What? No. I didn't know that. So, you're a peeping Tom?" He joked, "I better warn the neighbors."

Embarrassed that she had told on herself, she said, "No! It just happened that one time. And it wasn't my fault! It was an accident!"

He enjoyed Sara's attempt to redeem herself in his eyes.

She continued, "You remember that stupid smoke alarm went off?"

Humoring her, he said, "Uh huh."

"I yelled to get your attention. When you didn't answer, I walked into your room. I didn't realize you had clear shower doors until I stepped around the corner."

"Uh huh."

She insisted, "It wasn't my fault!"

Getting a kick out of the conversation, he asked, "So, as soon as you realized it, you turned away?"

Biting her bottom lip, she confessed, "Well, not exactly."

With an accusatory tone, he asked, "You watched, didn't you?"

Sara admitted, "Yes, I watched you take a shower. Now you think I'm a horrible person."

Phil laughed a hearty belly laugh. "No, honey, you're just normal and curious, like the rest of us."

CHAPTER 47

AFTER Tony changed the tire on Sully's sedan, he followed his parents and brother home from the safe house.

Rose was uncharacteristically quiet for the duration of the drive.

When they arrived home, Sal announced, "I can't tell you how relieved I am that that's over."

Tony replied, "Me too, Pop."

Joe said, "I'll call Helen to let her know everything is okay."

Rose responded, "Good idea. But before you do that, I have something to say to you."

"What?"

Rose said, "You know I want you with a nice girl, especially now that you have a daughter to raise. Right?"

Slumping into a chair, Joe whined, "Aw, geez, Ma, can we not do this now? Please? I'm tired, and I'm not ready."

Impatiently, she asked, "Will you let me finish?"

"Do I have a choice?"

"No. I want to say that I will not play matchmaker for you anymore. Unless you ask me to. In that case, then of course, I will. And I won't interfere with your other life choices either. You need to make your own decisions from now on. Unless you ask for my advice or opinion. Then, of course, I won't hesitate to help you."

Facetiously, Joe asked, "Did you fall and hit your head or something? Did someone brainwash you when we weren't looking? Who are you? And what have you done with my mother?"

"Cute, smart aleck. I'm fine."

"Can I get this in writing?"

She threatened, "Keep it up, and I'll change my mind."

Holding up his hands, he said, "No. I'll take your word for it." He stood up and hugged her. "Why the sudden change of heart?"

She acknowledged, "Well, I have to admit that Sara gave me something to think about."

The men looked at her stunned.

Rose complained, "Oh, don't you all give me that look. I can take constructive criticism."

Sal coughed. "There's a first time for everything."

Ignoring him, she continued, "While I was cleaning that godforsaken safe house, I had a lot of time to think. And she was right about a few things. So, there you have it."

Astounded, Joe said, "Wow! Thanks, Ma."

Rose added, "But if you want me to get involved or take over, you just say the word. And I'll take care of things for you."

Joe laughed. "Okay. I'll let you know, Ma."

Turning to her other son, Rose said, "Anthony, I want you to extend a dinner invitation to your task force teammates."

Tony questioned, "Really? After everything that happened, I thought you never wanted to see them again."

"Did you not hear anything I just said? Just do it."

"Okay."

"By the way, what kind of cake does Agent Ashby like?"

"I have no idea."

"Well, make sure to ask him."

CHAPTER 48

O N any other night, Rose might have invited the extended family to dinner. Under other circumstances, she might have waited for Flora and Helen to return. However, tonight, she felt compelled to keep the gathering centered around the guests.

The doorbell rang. Tony sprang up to answer it. He welcomed his fellow task force members.

They entered the house in single file behind Sully. Unsure of what to bring, each member brought a bottle of wine.

Sully helped Tony carry the bottles into the kitchen.

Rose busied herself by serving hors d'oeuvres.

Sully commented, "Looks like you're set on wine for a month or two."

Tony whispered, "Unless this dinner party goes badly. Then, we might have to drink it all just to make it until dessert."

Rejoining the others, Sully said, "Let's hope not."

White complimented Rose on the bacon-wrapped scallops, while the men took second helpings of the hors d-oeuvres.

Lee and Gupta discussed some new online game they discovered, as they enjoyed Rose's spinach and artichoke dip.

Ashby said to Joe, "If you want to learn how to shoot, I'll be at the range this week. I can teach you. There are usually some hot women practicing on Wednesdays."

"Dude, you spent way too much time with Ma. Did she put you up to this?"

Ashby replied, "Nah. You're the only one in the house who

doesn't know how to shoot. I was just trying to get you out of this house for a few hours."

Joe reconsidered, "In that case, count me in."

When Rose left the room to bring out more food, Spaulding joked, "Are we facing a firing squad?"

Tony laughed. "I have no idea. But at least you're getting fed first."

Spaulding replied, "Well, at least that's something. These appetizers are really good."

After dinner, but before dessert was served, Rose said, "I'd like to say something to our guests."

All eyes were fixed on Rose.

Rose cleared her throat. "As much grief as I gave all of you throughout this ordeal, I want to thank you for keeping my family safe. And considering what we all endured together, I consider you to be family now. My door is always open to all of you."

The team members exchanged surprised looks.

Sully spoke, "We understand how difficult this has been for you and your loved ones. On behalf on my team, we are honored to be part of your family. And we thank you for your hospitality and this fantastic meal."

"It was the least I could do for you. It was my pleasure. God bless you all, wherever you go from here."

Sal raised his glass. "*Salute!*"

His toast was echoed by all, "*Salute!*"

Rose smiled at her newly-extended family. "For dessert, I made a special cake for Agent Ashby. Who wants some delicious pineapple upside-down cake?"

CHAPTER 49

PHIL unlocked the front door to his house. With his good arm, he held the door for Sara. "Welcome to your new home."

Weary from the trip and the accompanying drama, Sara answered, "Thank you. When I'm with you, I feel like I'm home. Does that make sense?"

Closing the door behind him, he replied, "Yes. Completely."

Sara yawned.

He suggested, "It's late, and we're both tired. How about I get a fire started, and we curl up on the couch?"

Sara countered, "How about *I* get the fire started? The doctor told you that you can't bend over or lower your head for two weeks. You don't want any bleeding. So, no fire-making for you. Sit and relax."

"Are you going to be my nursemaid now?"

Placing the logs in optimal positions, she said, "For now, yes. But don't get used to it."

"Not even if I buy you a nurse's outfit?"

"Ha! Well, I might be persuaded to wear it on occasion."

"That reminds me, we need to buy one of those sex books. If you're not going to let me do anything around here, I could get a lot of reading done."

Sara struck a match and lit a piece of newspaper with it. She held the burning paper against the logs. They were dry, so they caught fire easily.

Satisfied, Sara sank into the comfortable couch cushions next to Phil. It already felt like home.

The fire crackled as the flames danced.

Sara sighed happily. "Mmm ..."

Since becoming intimate, their bodies effortlessly enmeshed when they cuddled. However, his injuries posed some challenges. After a few position changes, they settled in.

Snuggling, he said, "It seems fitting we're back where it all began."

Correcting him, Sara said, "Technically, we met in the diner."

He smirked. "In the diner, you were hellbent on getting away from me. And you really didn't want my help when you were stranded either. It was here, in this cabin, where you warmed up to me."

She teased, "I guess you're right. I mean, after I saw you naked, how could I resist?"

Their laughter gave way to tender kisses.

Gazing into his dreamy eyes, Sara said, "You really are something, Phil Potter."

Kissing her sweetly, he replied, "You are heaven on earth, sweetheart."

EPILOGUE

ONE Month Later – An orchestral recording of the classical piece, *Spring*, from Vivaldi's, *Four Seasons*, filled the cool, tranquil evening air. The sun set behind the mountains as soothing violins set the mood.

Phil stood under an archway crafted from interwoven branches and wildflowers found on his property. He wrapped the boughs with clear twinkling lights.

Phil wore a light gray suit with a white shirt, sans tie. His boutonniere was a single pink rose. His brother, Tommy, and the local preacher waited with him.

Sara checked off the mandatory wedding list in her head. *The something old is Anna's butterfly necklace. My something new is the dress. I'm wearing the something borrowed on my feet. And the something blue is the blue flowers. Guess I'm all set.*

Recently, it had rained. So, the natural aisle was still soggy and muddy.

Sara walked toward them wearing a simple, white chiffon sheath wedding dress and Tommy's light brown work boots. She carried a bouquet of pink roses, white Queen Anne's lace, yellow daisies, blue verbena, and pink cosmos, all tied with a white ribbon. A cluster of blue verbena was nestled in her dark brown hair.

With each step, the happiness within Sara grew. She felt like skipping down the aisle. Sara had never felt more alive than at this moment.

As she approached, Phil felt as if his heart would burst. *Sara has never looked more beautiful.* He wondered, *How did I get so lucky?*

Sara smiled the entire way down the aisle. When she joined Phil under the arch, he leaned over and kissed her.

The preacher joked, "You're getting a little ahead of yourself. You're supposed to do that at the end of the ceremony."

They all laughed.

After some opening remarks, the preacher said, "You have written your own vows. Now is the time for you to say them."

Looking into Sara's eyes, Phil professed, "Sara, I love you. When I am with you, I am home. Your presence makes me feel more alive than I've ever felt. Your sweet smile fills my heart to overflowing. I will move heaven and earth to make you happy. I promise to support you in all that you do. I also promise to be true to you, in good times and bad, for richer, or poorer, in sickness, and in health, and I'll even tolerate your bad footwear choices, all the days of my life."

Sara laughed. "Thanks, honey. Thanks a lot."

Phil winked at her.

The preacher prompted, "Sara, it's your turn."

Sara vowed, "Phil, I love you. When I am with you, I am home. I am grateful that you guided me to find the strength and courage within me to be myself again and pursue my dreams. That is the greatest gift anyone has ever given me. I will do everything I can to make sure you are happy and satisfied with our life together. I promise to be true to you, in good times and bad, for richer, or poorer, in sickness, and in health, all the days of my life."

Turning to Tommy, the preacher asked, "The rings?"

Producing the rings, Tommy replied, "I've got them, right here."

The preacher held Sara's bouquet while the couple exchanged rings.

After handing the bouquet back, the preacher declared, "By the power invested in me, by God and the State of New York, I now pronounce you husband and wife. Now, Phil, you may kiss your bride."

Phil dipped Sara and kissed her.

There were handshakes and hugs of congratulations amongst them.

Sara said, "We have a small cake and champagne."

Tommy said, "Well, I guess I need to make a toast then."

They walked over to the table. Phil poured champagne for the four of them.

Lifting his glass, Tommy said, "I've never seen my brother look happier than he does today. And I have to admit that I'm jealous. I hope to have what you guys have one day. Sara, welcome to the family. Good luck keeping him in line. I wish you both many, many years of love, health, and happiness."

The preacher said, "Hear, hear! To the happy couple!"

When he finished his glass of champagne, Phil said, "When are we cutting the cake? I'm hungry."

Sara laughed. "Why don't we do it now?"

"Perfect!"

Tommy took pictures while the happy bride and groom cut the cake and fed it to one another.

Shortly thereafter, it began to sprinkle.

Tommy said, "Well, at least the rain held out long enough to have the ceremony."

Sara agreed, "Yes. Thanks again for letting me borrow your boots. I'll clean them and get them back to you as soon as I can."

"You're welcome. No rush. You can even consider them a wedding present, if you'd like. Congrats again. I'm heading out before the deluge starts."

The preacher shook their hands. "Always a pleasure to be part of a loving couple's wedding day."

Phil responded, "Thank you again for coming all the way out here. I really appreciate it."

The preacher replied, "You're welcome. God bless you both."

Phil said, "Alone at last!"

Sara giggled as they walked, hand in hand back to the house.

Phil questioned, "Were you really okay with that small of a wedding?"

"You know, I always thought that I wanted a big wedding with hundreds of people. But after everything that has happened, I realized that's not what I wanted anymore. Our union is just that—our union. Just you and me. Sure, big parties are nice. But this was better."

"Really?"

"Yes! Instead of getting married in a stuffy church, we were married in our backyard. With our hands, we gathered the wood and fashioned the arch that will be on the property forever. And again, with our hands, we picked the wildflowers for my bouquet. What more could we have done to express our unity and our love? I'm so happy today that I don't even mind wearing Tommy's boots."

"Well, your pretty white shoes wouldn't have lasted a minute in that mud."

Sara agreed, "It was a make-it-work moment."

When they reached the front door, Phil opened the door and swept Sara up in his arms. "It's time to kick off those muddy boots."

In a flash, Sara kicked them off. She sighed happily and kissed her husband.

Phil asked, "Are you ready?"

Sara replied, "Ready!"

As Phil carried her across the threshold, he said, "Welcome home, Mrs. Potter."

Jubilant, she replied, "It's wonderful to be home, Mr. Potter."

He kicked the door closed. "I love you more than words can say."

"You know I feel the same way."

Kissing her neck, he said, "I hope you don't mind, but I plan to ravish you all night."

"Sounds wonderful. But I have a present for you to open first."

"A present? For me?"

"Yes. A wedding present."

"Can't it wait?"

"No. You have to open it now."

Curious, he put her down. "Okay. Where's this present?"

She opened the closet door and pulled out a large rectangular gift wrapped in wedding paper. "Here it is. Open it!"

Phil shook it. His effort was met with silence. He shook it again. Still nothing.

Sara urged, "Just open it!"

Phil winked at her. He peeled back the paper to reveal a deluxe edition of the *Kama Sutra*. "Oh! Just what I wanted! I'm really glad I didn't have to wait until Christmas to get this."

Sara giggled. "I'm so glad you like it."

"Honey, we're both going to *love* it. I bet there's even a money-back guarantee. Now, I have a surprise present for you."

Excitedly, Sara replied, "I love your surprises!"

Phil extended his hand. "Close your eyes, and follow me."

Eagerly, she interlocked her fingers with his. They walked through the house. She heard the sliding glass door in the master bedroom slide open.

Phil said, "Okay. You can open your eyes now."

On the patio sat a large, two-person hammock. It was identical to the hammock at their bungalow in Hawaii.

Amazed, she exclaimed, "Oh, Phil! You didn't!"

"As you can see, I did. I promised you plenty of frenzied romps on the hammock. And a Potter always keeps his promises."

Sara threw her arms around Phil's neck. "Well, then, let the honeymoon begin!"

ABOUT THE AUTHOR

Author, poet, and humorist, Suzanne Purewal, worked in the automotive industry for over two decades before her creative side decided that enough was enough. Since leaving Corporate America, she has published several books of different genres.

Her humorous book, *Mis-Matched to Miss Matched*, chronicles her hilarious and bizarre misadventures in online dating. As a follow-up, she co-authored, *Finally! An Unexpected Love Story*, with fellow author, L. E. Hewitt. Their quirky senses of humor will have you laughing out loud in this "He Said/She Said" book that follows their zany courtship.

The novels in her *Destiny* trilogy contain a mixture of mystery, romance, and humor that create exciting adventures for the characters and readers alike.

Suzanne's poetry book, *From 14 to 41*, contains a soulful blend of love, loss, whimsical, and inspirational pieces.

She has resided in Noblesville, IN for twenty-four years.

Suzanne loves to hear from her readers!

If you enjoyed this book, please review it
on Amazon, Barnes and Noble, or Goodreads!

Check out the latest news and events on Suzanne's website:
www.suzannepurewal.com

www.ingramcontent.com/pod-product-compliance
Lightning Source LLC
Chambersburg PA
CBHW071113100726
47908CB00008B/2360